Annie Laura's Triumph

Annie Laura's Triumph

MILINDA JAY

Mercer University Press | Macon, Georgia

2016

MUP/ P539

© 2016 by Mercer University Press
Published by Mercer University Press
1501 Mercer University Drive
Macon, Georgia 31207
All rights reserved

9 8 7 6 5 4 3 2 1

ISBN   978-0-88146-595-2
Cataloging-in-Publication Data is available from the Library of Congress

Do not remember the former things, or consider the things of old.
I am about to do a new thing; now it springs forth, do you not perceive it?
I will make a way in the wilderness and rivers in the desert.

—Isaiah 43:18–19 (NRSV)

To my dear cousin, Sandy Moore

Annie Laura's Triumph

Chapter 1

Grassy Glade, Florida, 1915

Annie Laura walked with purpose down the road surrounded by a gator-infested swamp, her black lace-up shoes sinking and taking on sand. She stopped, unlaced her shoes, sifted the sand between her fingers, and studied it through one squinted eye.

"Well, good," she said.

The whiter the sand, the closer she was to her firstborn.

Though only eight miles, it felt like the longest journey Annie Laura had ever made. She swatted a mosquito away from her face and adjusted the net of her Sunday straw hat so that it protected more than her eyes. She'd already walked half of the way, and the swelling in her ankles begged her to stop. "Now you just stop your complainin'," she said, as if the ankle was one of her young'uns, and she could shush it with a word.

In her thirty-eight years, she had walked longer distances. Was it age, the baby inside her, or dread that made the ankle pains come?

The late morning sun beat down, and the sound of the swamp rose to a deafening cry. She wanted to put her hands over her ears to drown out the crying. It was the sound of her baby being wrenched from her arms, her own sobs, her baby's screams, all happening in one terrifying moment. But that was almost sixteen years ago. What she heard today was only the cicadas and swamp insects.

She walked on, listening to the gators call to one another, hissing and rumbling, their bellows leaking bubbles into the still waters. Gators looked harmless, gliding along the water's surface, their black, glassy eyes watching. But Annie Laura had seen an old bull gator snatch a puppy wandering too close to shore. She could still hear the surprised yelp, see the alligator's flashing tail, the swirling water, and then nothing. She'd lunged forward to save the puppy, but her husband's strong hands held her back.

The memory caused Annie Laura to hurry through the swamp, walking as quickly as she could to get to the road where dry land lay on either side. She had looked forward to this day, and fear wasn't going to stop her from meeting her firstborn in the flesh. Annie Laura could still feel that sweet baby in her arms, the warm body, the tiny hands, the joy of seeing her first smile. For years she'd put it all behind her, but today she would hold her baby one more time. And, perhaps, make up for all of those lost years. Of course, the baby was almost a grown woman, nearly sixteen years old. She had to remember that and treat her as such.

The spring sun warmed away the early morning chill. Soon enough it would turn hot. Nothing like the summer, but hot enough. Annie Laura had been careful to choose just the right outfit when she'd dressed this morning. Thick wool socks to keep her feet warm and cushioned. A cotton petticoat, which would serve the dual purpose of keeping her warm in the morning and cool in the afternoon. On top of everything, she wore her best worsted-wool overskirt, the Sunday one, saved for weddings, funerals, and this, her twice-a-year journey to Grassy Glade, Florida.

In the past, she'd come to check up on Viola Lee. Annie Laura never saw her on those twice yearly visits, she just talked with an old friend who did. Today she would finally meet her. The cold wind of fear swept through her and she shivered. What if Viola Lee was angry at her for giving her up those many years ago? What if Viola Lee had agreed to meet her just to say she never wanted to have any contact with her ever again? What if this journey ended in a final estrangement?

An outsider might laugh at those words. *Annie Laura, how can you estrange a child who doesn't even live with you, who doesn't even know you?*

Her answer would be this: Easy. The secret she needed to share with Viola Lee just might do it. Would she have the courage to tell her daughter the real reason she had given her up?

Do not remember the former things, or consider the things of old. I am about to do a new thing; now it springs forth, do you not perceive it? The verse from Isaiah came to mind and allowed her to ignore the

2

nauseating thrust of memory. She focused on the hope that came with new beginnings. She wiped away the paralyzing memory, replaced it with the vision before her, the new green leaves, the tiny purple and yellow wildflowers, the gentle spring breeze.

She peered down the seemingly endless sandy road. She was almost to the end of the swamp.

A little bit farther down she saw what appeared to be a log, reaching from one side of the road to the other, like a bridge across the swamp. It was a strange sight as there were no tall trees near enough to fall just this way. Why would someone set a log in the middle of the road?

Maybe her glasses needed adjusting. She squinted and shaded her eyes to see better. It looked like a burned-black log, maybe an ancient pine. As she drew closer, she could see that the log tapered on either end, and that the center was wide enough to sit on comfortably. It looked inviting, but she needed to get to Grassy Glade in time to catch the noon ferry. Soon as she reached the log, she would have to climb over it and pass it on by.

An unexpected breeze rustled through the cypress trees and stirred the sandy dust on the road. It swirled around the log. Annie Laura stopped. She squinted at the log again. This close, it didn't look so much like a burnt pine tree.

She felt the heat course through her body.

The log wasn't a log at all. It was a gator. Annie Laura backed a safe distance away.

She rolled up both her sleeves and thought about walking back home, but that meant shutting the window of the short but precious time she had with her daughter. Besides, home was a long way away, and Pappy—the kind neighbor who had given her a ride all the way to the crossroads—wasn't due back until an hour past sunset. She didn't want to hear her husband, Leonard, chasten her about the foolishness of this visit. He didn't think much of her coming down to Grassy Glade to see Viola Lee. He said it was best to leave well enough alone. Annie Laura thrust her hand into her pocket and rubbed the fine linen handkerchief her daughter, Louise, had embroidered for Viola Lee's wedding day. The feel of the carefully wrought gift comforted her.

The gator slept peacefully oblivious in the warm sun.

Annie Laura stood, uncertain what to do next. Normally, gators got scared when humans walked close. But this one seemed not to have noticed her. She sat down in the sand a safe distance away and rested her tired feet. She listened to the drone of cicadas in the swamp, the hiss of gators, the roiling bubbles. Precious time slipped away. The big gator might as well be a statue.

Now, Lord, she prayed, *you've gotten me through some tight spots in my life. I reckon you'll get me through this one. You just let me know what it is you think I ought to do, and I'll do it.*

She waited. The gator did not move. What if sudden noise or movement on her part made the gator aggressive? She stood slowly and backed away a few more paces.

The defiant scream of a red-tailed hawk scared her so bad she could hear her heart thrum in her ears. She pitched forward, but caught herself before falling. She breathed deeply and watched the hawk dive down into the swamp and emerge with a small creature between its talons. She couldn't make out what it was—a baby rabbit? The hawk flew up into the sky, lurching a little with his burden. She looked for his nest and spotted the bulky structure at the top of a tall cypress tree.

Would Viola Lee wait for her if she was late? She couldn't abandon her again. Even if this time wasn't Annie's fault, it would feel like it was to Viola Lee. Would Viola Lee ever forgive her?

Did she deserve forgiveness? The thought smacked her in the head and laid her out. She buried the thought as quick as it came.

And what of home? What about her other children? Did they miss her? She couldn't help but feel a small relief at being away for the day—no washing, no cleaning, no planting, no plowing.

And no husband to deal with. Well, she had made a pledge, and she would keep it. But it was growing increasingly difficult. What happened to the sweet man she married?

She knew Louise, her oldest child at home, would take care of things. She was a good girl, her Louise. Annie Laura hated leaving her with all the responsibility of her little brothers and sisters, but Louise understood, had encouraged her to go and check on Viola Lee. Louise didn't know that Annie Laura was meeting Viola Lee face to face for the first time.

The smell of the swamp—dank, mossy, and rotten—assailed her nostrils. She felt queasy, like she might throw up her breakfast biscuit and ham. She swallowed, closed her eyes, and forced herself to think of a cool spring and the smell of summer jasmine. It didn't help her nausea a whit, but it did make her feel a little cooler.

Surely a car or wagon would happen along soon. A mosquito landed on her arm. She wanted to slap it but feared the noise would alert the gator to her presence, and he would charge her. She knew it wasn't likely, but still, she smashed the mosquito quietly with the palm of her hand, rubbing the black and red goo onto her bare arm. She reached down for some sandy dirt to clean it off.

Waiting was hard. She was normally a patient person, but her time was short for this visit. Pappy would be picking her up sooner than she wished.

Meanwhile, it was her and this gator.

Well, she had faced adversaries before. *And been defeated by them.* Not defeated, she replied to that part of herself that wanted to weigh her down. Not defeated. Just temporarily put out of commission. Past was best left in the past.

And, besides, look at what she had done since. She'd built a whole new life. And now was the time to repair past damage as best she could. No longer would she be an onlooker in her firstborn's life. No. Today, she was going to meet her in the flesh and talk to her.

The gator snoozed on. She wished there was a way to walk around it, but there wasn't enough room on either end of the eight-foot gator for her to safely navigate without taking a swim in the swamp.

Well, this was a fine fix. She wasn't afraid of the gator, not as long as he was sleeping. What she was afraid of was not having enough time to spend with Viola Lee.

But what would she tell her daughter? How would she explain? Leonard told her she was a fool to keep checking up on Viola Lee.

She'd hidden their correspondence from him.

"She ain't yours anymore," he'd said. "And when she finds out the truth about how you gave her up—"

"Stop it!" Annie Laura said. "You don't know the truth."

"Do you?" Leonard asked.

She felt the ground rumble. She sat stock-still. The alligator flashed its tail, back and forth, rubbing a fan-shaped design into the sand. It rose up on its short legs, claws extended.

Annie Laura held her breath. *Please, Lord, let it go on out into the swamp where it belongs.*

A Model-T Ford chugged down the road, its driver leaning out the window, his driving goggles dust-covered, his long scarf flaring behind him.

He tooted his horn, and then chugged to a stop beside Annie Laura.

The gator flicked his tail again and stayed right where he was.

The driver lifted his driving goggles and peered over at Annie Laura, then the gator, and back to Annie Laura again.

"Well, Annie Laura Seymour," he said jovially, "looks like you and me are in a bit of a tight."

Annie Laura smiled, but panic filled her. Of all the people to have stopped. She was thankful for help, but she would appreciate it if it had been someone she didn't know, or, at least, not the adoptive father of her firstborn child. How was she going to explain being here? It was John Sebring who kept her up to date on Viola Lee. John Sebring whom she came to meet twice a year to get news of Viola Lee's growing up. She would have to tell him the truth. She meant to meet her child. Today.

John Sebring Morgan leaned over and opened the passenger's side. The half door swung open. "Come on," he said. "Hop on in while we wait this ole gator out."

"Thank you kindly, John Sebring," she said in her most grateful voice. She squeezed out the quaver of panic.

"How long you been waiting here for this big old granddaddy gator to move? I reckon he could just sit out here all day. What else does he have to do? Now I myself have some picnickers to pick up in Grassy Glade and haul over to the ferry so they can spend this beautiful day on the island. But if this here gator doesn't move soon, I'm going to lose today's business, and you know how Mary Scarlett feels about that."

John Sebring was long on words and short on patience, and for this Annie Laura was thankful. Maybe she wouldn't have to explain herself at all. Maybe he would keep up a running stream of conversation until the gator moved and she was safely deposited at the county pier.

The scent of fresh-caught fish wafted through the air. Annie Laura looked into the back seat of the sedan to see a bucket full of bream. John Sebring knew the best fishing holes in three counties. He never came home empty-handed, or so Viola Lee said about her adopted daddy.

"That's a nice mess of fish you got back there, John Sebring."

"Thank you, but Mary Scarlett don't appreciate 'em so much. She wishes they were dollar bills."

"Well, I reckon you save a lot of dollar bills with all the fish you catch," Annie Laura said.

"Viola Lee likes them fine," John Sebring said, "but Mary Scarlett only likes gulf fresh fish. And who goes gulf fishing? Not me. I don't trust the waves."

Annie Laura nodded and tried to think of something to say to keep the conversation going. She didn't want him asking her any more questions about what she was up to.

At that moment he gunned the Model T and moved right up to the alligator.

The gator didn't pay the least bit of attention to the Ford.

"Now I'm thinking I might nudge this here gator. If he don't move soon, not only am I going to lose my business, but my fish aren't going to be fit for eating."

The gator lay before them, still as a possum.

"He'll be looking for his girlfriend soon enough," John said hopefully.

They were both quiet so long that Annie Laura felt her eyelids growing heavy. The walk had been a long one, and she'd risen early to milk the cows, gather the eggs, and prepare food for the children she left at home.

"You know any tricks for getting gators off the road?" John Sebring asked, jolting her awake.

Annie Laura sat up straight and shook her head. "No," she said. "Never had to think of it before."

"I've never known an alligator to just set here like this. Usually my car scares 'em off."

Annie Laura nodded in agreement.

"I've got an idea," John said.

He reached into the car and grabbed the bucket of fresh fish. He pulled one out and threw it a couple of feet in front of the gator.

The gator roused itself, rose up on his short legs, darted forward with astonishing speed, opened and snapped close massive jaws. The fish was gone. John threw another closer to the edge of the swamp. The gator snapped it up. Then he threw another and another, each fish leading the gator closer to the water and off the road. The gator snapped up every one. Annie Laura watched the gator glide into the swamp and out into the murky green water, his dark gray body glistening with water droplets, shimmering in the bright morning sun.

John Sebring jumped back into the car before the gator changed his mind and camped back out on the road.

"I'm sorry you had to use up most of your fish," Annie Laura said.

"Glad to get shed of them," John said. "My paying customers might not appreciate the smell." For the first time, John Sebring seemed to focus on Annie Laura. "Where are you heading, Annie Laura?" John's normally friendly eyes had become suddenly guarded.

Annie Laura cleared her throat. "In town for some business, looking to catch the noon ferry," she said.

She studied him. The set of his lips told her he was not satisfied with her answer.

Could she trust the man who had loved her daughter since she was born, and raised her as his own?

The car rattled over the bumpy dirt road, lurching this way and that. Annie Laura held on to her straw hat to keep it from flying out the half door.

"Well, it's a right nice day to visit the island," he said, and this time, she knew he was fishing for information. "You going alone?"

"No," she said shortly. She couldn't keep her secret from John Sebring. He had been like a brother to her since she was a girl. He and his second wife, Mary Scarlett, had raised Viola Lee. "You might as well know, I've arranged to meet Viola Lee there."

"You meeting with her out in public?" John asked, his forehead creased with concern.

"I am. I've made up my mind, John Sebring, and I'm not to be talked out of it. I'm not ashamed, and Viola Lee shouldn't be either. She's had to bear the burden of 'illegitimate' on her birth certificate her whole life. I know she's been shunned in some homes, and it's not her fault. She deserves the truth."

"Which truth you talking about?" John Sebring asked evenly. "Yours or ours?"

"I hope they're one and the same."

"Truth doesn't work like that. You of all people should know."

"I'm going to say my truth, John Sebring. You can say yours."

"And Mary Scarlett?"

"I imagine she's been filling Viola Lee's head with her truth since Viola Lee was old enough to listen." Why John Sebring had married Mary Scarlett was beyond Annie Laura's reckoning. Perhaps it had been out of the desperation born of loneliness and loss. Whatever the outcome of this day the town gossips would carry to the front porch of Mary Scarlett's dry goods store.

John's forehead wrinkled. "But why this day?" he asked. "This has something to do with the wedding, doesn't it? You worried about her marrying too young?"

"No," she said, though John Sebring was partially right. Viola Lee was getting married, and she wanted to hear about it, but not from somebody else. Was it selfish to want her daughter to tell her about her wedding? "I just want to hear about it is all. And I want her to tell me."

"The groom needs to show up for there to be a wedding," he said.

Annie's heart lurched. "You think he might not come?"

"I know he loves her, but he was supposed to be here a week ago."

Surely Viola Lee's groom would show up on her wedding day.

Annie Laura gathered her skirts and felt for her bag.

"I appreciate your showing up in time to get rid of the gator, John."

John laughed. "That was the biggest damn gator I've ever seen in my life." He looked across at her, then reddened. "I'm sorry," he said.

"No offense taken," Annie Laura said. She knew he was used to talking loose around Mary Scarlett, who didn't have any use for church ways. "Thank you kindly, John." Annie Laura reached out a gloved hand, and squeezed John's strong hand. She looked into his blue eyes, and a lump rose in her throat.

"It's been sixteen years, nearly seventeen, and I miss your Maggie and the baby every day of my life. She was the best friend I've ever had."

They'd nearly reached the ferry dock, and John looked away out over the sparkling waters of North Bay to the sleepy little town of Bay Haven. A few miles beyond lay the vast Gulf of Mexico. "I know," he said as if yearning could take him there.

"You're doing a right nice job of keeping her grave clean, hers and the baby's. I go visit it sometimes when I'm up that way."

John Sebring didn't say anything, just nodded. He swiped at his eye.

"Here." Annie Laura reached into her bag and pulled out a ham-filled biscuit. "You eat this. It's sure to make you feel better."

John laughed. "You're always feeding folks, Annie. And there ain't nothin' better than your biscuits. I can taste it now."

"Well put it in your mouth so you can taste it for real. Stop this car. You go on ahead and drop me here. I can walk the rest of the way. It's not far, and you need to get your customers." Annie Laura stepped out of the car and looked back at John.

He wiped a biscuit crumb from his mouth. "I aim to get an angel statue," John said, his voice gruff. "Two of them. One for her and one for the baby."

"That'd be real nice. I know Maggie would like that."

"I don't understand why the good ones go first."

"Me neither, John Sebring, me neither."

"And I don't understand why the mean ones are allowed to go on wreaking their violence, ruining lives." His hands gripped the steering wheel. "What kind of God allows a man like Walter Blakely to stay alive when my Margaret is gone?"

Annie Laura shivered at the naming of the man who had broken her nearly perfect world. "I don't know," she said. She reached across the seat and patted his arm. "We'll get through," she said. "And one day, we'll get an answer to our questions. Until then, I pray for peace for the both of us."

"Do you get peace, ever, after all that's happened to you?"

Annie Laura smiled. "I do. When it gets real bad, I try to hush my mind and think on my blessings."

"Well," John Sebring said, "sometimes I get peace when I'm out on the lake fishing or sitting in the woods waiting. I hear the birds and see the sky and the trees outlined against it. You ever noticed how beautiful the new green of a pine tree is against a clear blue spring sky?"

"I'll be looking for that today."

John Sebring nodded. "I hope to see you soon, Annie Laura. You always did do my heart good."

The cool bay breeze swirled around Annie Laura. She held her hat firmly on her head and waved goodbye to her friend. She turned and made her way down the sandy, sea-oat-lined path leading to the ferry. The steamer stood like a proud citadel in the smooth waters of North Bay. When she'd paid her money and stepped on, her heart did a little leap.

Chapter 2

A young girl stood on the other side of the ferry, her hands on the railing, her white hat tied firmly with a gauzy bow. It had to be Viola Lee. Annie Laura's heart beat hard.

Could she do it? Could she tell her daughter the truth? Or would the truth break Viola Lee's heart? The letters they'd exchanged had been friendly. But what could you tell from a letter? Annie Laura had to walk across the ferry deck and close the gap between them—the final leg of the sixteen-year journey. She gathered her courage in one hand and her belongings in the other.

She gazed at her daughter. Viola Lee was beautiful. Tiny, like a little doll, her soft, brown hair gathered into a loose bun, her white dress shining in the noon sun. Her dress was lawn linen, with dainty hand embroidery, inset lace, and an underslip of the same.

Whatever else you might say about Mary Scarlett Morgan—who seemed more interested in building her business than she did in raising her adopted child—she was always careful to dress Viola Lee in beautiful clothes, hand-sewn by herself. Perhaps she sewed painstakingly gorgeous outfits for Viola Lee because she favored her as a walking advertisement for the lovely imported fabric she carried in her store. Or, perhaps it was Mary Scarlett's only way of expressing love. She was an otherwise hard woman. Whatever the reason, it made Annie Laura proud to see Viola Lee dressed so pretty, and, perhaps, lovingly.

Annie Laura looked down at her own outfit. Would Viola Lee be ashamed to be seen with her? Her Sunday best was a sad reminder of the gap between them. She clutched the straw hat and hoped that Viola Lee would recognize the red bow they'd agreed upon. What if there was another woman with a red bow around her straw hat? Annie Laura looked around. No, the women on this ferry all had white bows and ribbons, fitting for the season.

Just a few more steps. Would Annie Laura throw her arms around her child? Would she lift her and swirl her about as she had her other babies?

Would someone recognize her and try and stop her? Annie Laura put an anxious hand on her hat and pulled it closer to shade her face. There were too many prying eyes. Annie Laura must wait until the new passengers from the St. Andrews docks crowded the deck on their way to the island before she could greet Viola Lee properly.

Just then, Viola Lee turned toward her. Her smile upon recognizing Annie Laura was better than the bright spring sun. Annie Laura felt her throat swell, felt the tears form in her eyes. One escaped, making its way down her prematurely weatherworn face. Her thoughts switched from English to her native tongue, the German she hadn't spoken since she was a fifteen-year-old girl, new to this country. She'd forced herself to think in English at her mother's death when she knew to make it in this country she had to assimilate. She shook her head as if shaking would cast the German away.

Viola Lee looked away, and cast her eyes nervously around her.

Was she changing her mind?

Annie Laura waited, just a few steps away, while the ferry docked at the St. Andrews Marina and a whole new group of ferry passengers filed on, came between them, eager to get to the island to spend a day on the beach. She wanted to push them all out of the way; she needed to be able to see Viola Lee, make certain she hadn't changed her mind.

Instead, Annie Laura forced herself to watch as a family on holiday—mother, father, and three tow-headed boys—climbed aboard. The father carried a straw picnic basket, the mother a large crocheted bag with towels and swim trunks spilling out. The boys all wore identical long-sleeved, white lawn linen shirts and blue button-up shorts, the father a white linen coat and matching trousers. The mother, like Viola Lee, wore a white linen dress with an embroidered overlay, and a large white sun hat tied with an organdy ribbon. She reached out, keeping her youngest from climbing the ferry rails and falling overboard. The eldest, probably eight years old, grabbed the youngest boy's hand. The child jerked his hand away, but the mother scolded him, and he allowed his brother to keep him off the enticing side rail.

Annie Laura prayed that Viola Lee could, one day, have just such a family. Her own children at home had no experience with snow-white lawn linen. Instead, they wore chambray shirts, overalls, and the serviceable straw hats necessary for a day working the fields in the blistering Florida heat.

The decision Annie Laura had made sixteen years ago saved this, her eldest child, from that fate. That's what she had to tell herself.

The last passenger entered the ferry, a man whose face Annie Laura could not see, his Texas hat wide, its brim shading his face. He, too, was dressed in a white linen suit, ready for a day in the unrelenting sun. There was something about the man that made the hair stand up on the back of Annie Laura's neck. Some men affected her in this way. She squelched the feeling as foolish.

Annie Laura wondered why the man was alone. He didn't carry tackle for fishing. Perhaps he was a poet, eager to capture the beauty of the gulf, or was, like Annie, meeting someone.

The passenger gate clanged shut, the deckhand loosened the ties that bound the steamboat to the dock, the engine chugged, the water swirled, and the ferry boat lurched away from the dock and toward the island. The enormous North Bay separated the tiny communities dotting the coast. The ferry tied them together.

A gull shrieked above, beckoning them across the azure bay and out toward the open gulf waters. The whistle of the steamboat sounded a sharp reply. Annie Laura flinched.

Viola Lee had already taken the final step across the deck to Annie Laura. She placed a small, soft hand in Annie Laura's rough one, and squeezed. Annie Laura smiled, her throat tightened, and Viola Lee threw herself into Annie Laura's arms.

They stood this way for a while, mother and daughter, arms locked as if fearful of being torn apart. Annie Laura's hat shaded them both.

"Your hug feels like home. I wish this day could last forever."

Annie Laura laughed. "But it's only just now begun," she said. She stopped the words, *nothing lasts forever,* words she would have used with the rest of her children, the children she got to see every day, and said instead, "I have teacakes." She held out a small packet she'd kept safely tucked in one of her skirt pockets.

"Oh, Mama!" Viola Lee blushed and looked up into Annie Laura's face, checking to see if it was acceptable if she called her "Mama."

Annie Laura smiled. She looked into those trusting blue eyes and knew that she would not be able to do it. She had hoped Viola Lee might be polite, but had prepared herself for anger, just in case. She hadn't expected this overwhelming, non-judgemental, unconditional love. She could not tell Viola Lee the truth, not today. She needed to wait until they had spent some time together, gotten to know each other. Viola Lee deserved to know the truth, but she did not deserve to have her trust shattered. Not here. Not like this.

Viola Lee reached in for the soft teacakes. Her hands were shaking. She unwrapped the clean cloth from one, and crammed it immediately into her mouth, the crumbs scattering across the lawn linen like pollen. Annie Laura stopped herself from saying, *Save the dessert until you've eaten your lunch,* the words she would have used with her other children. Instead, she watched with joy as Viola Lee licked her fingers, smiled up at Annie Laura, and said, "Thank you so much! Teacakes are my favorite!"

"Doesn't Mary Scarlett bake for you?" Mary Scarlett had never known what it was like to clear a field nor aid in the birthing of a calf. Annie Laura herself would bake every day if the farm didn't take so much work. Baking was a luxury, something she did when she had the energy to stay up late into the night, when she wanted to surprise her children with a rare and unexpected sweet. She expected Mary Scarlett had plenty of time to cook.

"No, ma'am. Mother is too busy with the store. Sometimes my daddy helps. I do the rest." Viola Lee's lips set in a straight line, ever so briefly.

Was that bitterness? Annie Laura felt her heart give a little happy leap. And then she chided herself. This was not a contest. She was not here to prove herself the better mother.

"Well, I bet you're a mighty fine hand at cooking, then," Annie Laura had to stop feeling so judgmental toward Mary Scarlett. Hadn't she raised this beautiful girl for her? And Mary Scarlett worked hard, too. Annie Laura felt ashamed of herself and vowed to think on the good, even about Mary Scarlett.

"Some say so," Viola Lee blushed.

"I take it James has tasted your cooking and wants to sit at your table for the rest of his born days!"

Viola Lee laughed and the blush traveled down her neck, making her cornflower-blue eyes brighten. Annie Laura waited for her to say something about James not showing up for his wedding week, maybe explaining why. Perhaps she knew more about why he'd not yet shown up than she had told John Sebring.

"Yes, ma'am. He did say something like that to me."

Annie Laura waited, and when Viola Lee did not elaborate, she continued with the light conversation. "What's his favorite?"

"Roast beef. He loves my roast beef and gravy."

Annie Laura nodded. "I'd like to taste some of that roast beef one day."

"You will. When I have a house of my own, you can come visit any time you want, and I hope you will."

Annie Laura smiled and prayed it would be so easy. But there was something overly eager in Viola Lee's manner; she seemed almost too eager to accept Annie Laura with open arms. Didn't she have questions? Annie Laura squelched her doubt and forced herself to relax.

They stood, side by side, the wind whipping their skirts and the bright sun blinding them. The sound of the water churning blended with the sound of the steam engine pumping and wheezing, the stack blowing smoke in the air, leaving a trail of tiny, puffy gray clouds behind them. Annie Laura looked down at the water for a moment hoping to relieve her sun-strained eyes, but there was little relief there. The water shone an even brighter reflection of the sun.

Annie Laura closed her eyes for a moment, willing herself to be thankful for this moment, this day.

Footsteps sounded on the wood deck. A man walked up beside her, rested his hands on the rail. He was uncomfortably close.

Annie Laura looked down to see the flash of a diamond ring. She turned to Viola Lee, who was oblivious to the man, and saw the refracted light from the man's diamonds dancing across the front of Viola Lee's lawn linen.

The man was too close to look up into his face without seeming rude. Annie Laura moved away from the man and protectively closer to Viola Lee. She didn't like the way he was crowding her. The back of her neck prickled, and a warning bell went off in her head.

"Annie Laura, fancy meeting you here. I take it your whoring days are over?" he said, conversationally, staring straight out at the water as if he were more fascinated by the maneuverings of a pelican as it dipped into the sparkling water and rose with a fresh fish in its mouth than the effect of his words.

Annie Laura took in a sharp breath. She gripped the rail to keep from shaking and forced herself to look up and study the man whose face appeared only in her nightmares.

She had to be strong for Viola Lee. She would not show fear. The frightened girl she had been was long gone.

Age had not been kind to Walter Blakely. Beneath the wide-brimmed hat was a red-faced man, the veins on his nose and the tremor in his hands evidence of a life of hard drinking. Some might think him still handsome. She did not.

She straightened her posture and widened her shoulders. She glanced at Viola Lee, who had shrunk into herself, shoulders hunched, arms crossed, desperately squeezing her own waist.

Annie Laura shook her head, took a deep, steadying breath that came out like a sigh, and said evenly but loudly, "If I had a pistol, I'd use it. As it turns out, I don't. And that's probably for the best. I'd be hard-pressed to provide for my children from the county jail."

She enjoyed Blakely's surprise at her response. He jerked his chin towards her, and she held his gaze, her voice steel. "Speaking of jail, how did you get out? I thought you were standing trial up in Dothan?"

Blakely chuckled. "Out on bail. Money buys justice. You of all people should know that."

Once again, Walter Blakely skirted the law. The reckoning she believed had finally come for this man had not.

He turned his attention to Viola Lee. His hand clamped down on her arm, pressing it against the steamboat railing.

"What about Viola Lee here, marrying her own brother? You reckon that's a punishable offense?"

Viola Lee gasped, jerked her arm away. "Whatever would make you say such a vile thing?" she asked, rubbing her arm. "I don't even know you."

Annie Laura stepped between them.

"Stay away from her, Walter," Annie Laura said, louder than she had intended. What could he mean?

Walter Blakely laughed out loud, turned, and disappeared into the stairwell leading to the lower deck.

Annie Laura felt Viola Lee's eyes on hers, wide and questioning.

Had Walter Blakely raped others? Had he populated the area with misbegotten waifs?

The families milling leisurely about the deck fell silent. The mother with the over-stuffed bag of beach rugs and her husband with the picnic basket pulled their wide-eyed boys away from the scene. Annie Laura heard the boys protest.

"But, Mama," one said, "the dolphins have just begun following the wake." And the other whined, "I want to watch the dolphins jump, Mama. Please."

"Hush now," the mother said. "We'll watch the dolphins below deck through the windows."

The children voiced their protest, and the mother reached into their commodious bags and pulled out penny candy. "I'll give it to you as soon as you've seated yourself respectably below deck."

The boys were silenced.

Annie Laura looked around. She trembled and grasped the rail again for support. The only passengers left were those too close to the engine to have heard any of their words.

Except Viola Lee, who stood gripping the bar, her cheeks a splotchy red.

"That man was crazy. The look in his eyes reminded me of my dog when it got rabies. And why would he say such things to you? What does he know about James? I don't believe him," she said, and wrapped her arms around Annie Laura as if she were a life preserver and they were both drowning in the stormy gulf.

"I know. But he's gone now." Annie Laura relished the warmth of her child's embrace. How she had longed for these arms, how she had wished a hundred times to be able to hold her child, now a woman, in her arms.

Viola Lee nestled against her. She was a little, delicate thing, just like her sister Louise. Annie Laura was a strong woman, hardened by her years in the field. But the hands that Annie Laura held were not soft. They were chapped and red, a housewife's hands. She took the little rough hands in her own and held them tight. "I've longed for this day. We won't let him ruin it." Tears slipped down her cheeks.

"But why would he say such a thing?"

"I don't know, child."

Viola Lee studied Annie Laura's eyes. She looked down the deck where Walter Blakely had disappeared, and back at Annie Laura. Her brow furrowed.

Annie Laura had the sudden, sick fear that Viola Lee knew more.

The steamboat chugged its way across the bay, pulled up to the island dock, and deposited the afternoon picnickers on the shore.

"I reckon they are in for a day of fun," Annie Laura pointed to the passengers and hoped Viola Lee might focus on the passengers rather than Walter.

Viola Lee nodded and smiled a half smile, her eyes far away.

Viola Lee and Annie Laura watched them scamper off and head for the white dunes and the sparkling aqua gulf.

They waited as they exchanged places with the morning picnickers who loaded onto the steamboat, their bathing trunks damp from early morning swims, their faces pink from the sun. Annie Laura would love to take Viola Lee and the rest of her children on a picnic one day.

She had wanted this first meeting with her daughter to be on the water; she wanted the freedom of the blue sky and the sparkling bay. She wanted Viola Lee to remember that first day surrounded with beauty.

She had not counted on an encounter with Walter Blakely.

The boat was full now, and the steamboat chugged its way away from the island and back to the city shore.

"Maybe next time," Viola Lee said, "we can take us a picnic." Her blue eyes shone.

"Maybe," Annie Laura said, relieved. "Just maybe."

"Today is a perfect day. I'm here with you, my real mother." There was a mixture of defiance and pain in her tone.

A warning bell went off in Annie Laura's head. Viola Lee seemed eager, almost too eager to claim Annie Laura as her own.

Was it Walter Blakely's appearance that made her feel cautious about Viola Lee's energetic passion for her? Or was it that she had seen this overweening zeal in her own teenaged daughter, that desire to find a woman other than her own mother, Annie Laura, to adore. What was it about adolescence that made a girl suddenly realize the mother she adored was, in truth, a flesh-and-blood woman with real flaws? And how long did it take for the girl to resign herself to her mother's flaws and love her in spite of them?

Annie Laura decided that for now, even though it may simply be Viola Lee's mood, and short-lived, she would enjoy being the favored mother.

Annie Laura squeezed Viola Lee's hand, willing away the memory of Walter Blakely. He would not ruin her perfect day.

"Yes," Annie Laura said. "It is a perfect day. I just wish we had longer."

They held hands as the boat pulled away from the dock and chugged its way across the bay. The crossing was smooth, and the boat pulled up to the moorings, lurched forward and back as it found the pilings. The squeaking of the gangplank mixed with the squawking seagulls hoping for a bit of bait. But the gulls were disappointed and confused. This wasn't a fishing vessel, but a pleasure boat.

Annie Laura and Viola Lee waited while the people in front of them walked down the gangplank onto the city docks.

Blakely appeared at Annie Laura's elbow. He smiled and tipped his white hat. "Did you tell her you traded her for a piece of land?"

Chapter 3

Mary Scarlett—as Viola Lee had begun thinking of her adoptive mother—squeezed her lips tightly together the moment Viola Lee entered the room. The quilting pins she held between her lips flared like porcupine quills. Mary snatched one pin after the other from between her lips, forcing the quilt layers together with brutal stabs.

When her mouth was empty, she spoke to Viola Lee without turning. "I needed your help, but I suppose you were too busy with that woman."

How did Mary Scarlett know that she had been with Annie Laura? Viola Lee reached into her pocket and clutched the lovely handkerchief embroidered by her half-sister, Louise. It gave her strength.

"Her name is Annie Laura," Viola Lee said and walked to her bedroom. Had someone seen her already and reported directly to Mary Scarlett? She thought back over the afternoon. There had been no familiar faces on the ferry. None. She had checked. How, then, did she know? She couldn't imagine Annie Laura asking permission. She was pretty sure Mary Scarlett wouldn't have granted it if she'd been asked.

How, then?

She wouldn't give Mary Scarlett the pleasure of her own curiosity. She would pretend that she didn't care.

Besides, she had a lot more to think about than how Mary Scarlett had found out she was visiting with her real mother.

What had that crazed man meant when he said her mother had traded her for land? Was it true? Her mother's face had turned the white of Viola Lee's lawn linen, and the man had smirked as his heavy feet pounded down the gangplank and onto dry land.

But the man was a liar. Viola Lee knew this. After all, he had said that James was her brother. What a ridiculous tale. And he had grabbed her like he had a right to do so.

Who was he? He hadn't properly introduced himself, further indication of the sort of person he was. Viola Lee hadn't caught his name—something like "Blakely." What she had noticed was the fear and anger in Annie Laura's face when she recognized him.

Viola Lee smoothed the wrinkles from her lawn linen frock and changed into her everyday gingham. She pulled her apron from its hook beside the door, reached back to tie her bow, and reappeared in the kitchen to get supper ready. "Is there something I can help you with besides supper?" she asked Mary Scarlett, hoping to kill her with kindness.

"Why, aren't *you* just so sweet that sugar wouldn't melt in your mouth?"

Viola Lee chewed on the inside of her lip before responding.

"I'm happy to help you if you need help," Viola Lee said and made her way into the kitchen.

The truth was, Viola Lee wanted Mary Scarlett's help. Mary Scarlett probably knew Blakely and could explain things to her, like what the man had meant by saying she was about to marry her brother. And why had he called her mother a whore?

"I don't need help any more. It's too late. I did it all myself, as I usually do."

The petulant set to Mary Scarlett's lips was familiar. It would be of no use to ask her for help in unraveling the truth about her birth mother. "Why you would spend a moment with the woman who abandoned you is beyond my imagining," Mary Scarlett continued.

"Well, I did. And I enjoyed every minute of it." That was a lie. She had enjoyed meeting her mother, but the meeting had raised more questions than it had answered.

But she would not let Mary Scarlett see her pain or guess at her doubts. She would keep those to herself.

"Did anyone see you together who recognized her?" Mary Scarlett asked.

"Just one," Viola Lee replied. Of course Mary Scarlett must have known that. Otherwise, how could she know Viola Lee had met Annie Laura?

"Well, all it takes is one," Scarlett said, grimacing. "I suppose I'll have to live with that all week, then. Every woman in town will come by the shop to tell me they're praying for me, when really all they want is an update on how I'm reacting to my daughter spending time with that woman."

"I don't think you'll have to worry about this person," Viola Lee said. "It was a man."

"Well, he'll be sure to tell his wife."

"No," Viola Lee said. "I don't think so."

Scarlett narrowed her eyes. "There's something you're not telling me. Who was this man? What did he say to you?" she asked.

"He said I was getting ready to marry my brother and asked my moth—Annie Laura how she felt about that." The words spilled out.

Something more akin to fear than accusation appeared on Mary Scarlett's face.

Viola Lee felt the solid ground beneath her crumble.

"That's ridiculous," Mary Scarlett said. "Who was the man?" Mary Scarlett's voice had grown hoarse. "Someone must know."

"I don't know," Viola Lee said. "I've never seen him in my life. But Annie Laura said something about him being a Blakely." Viola Lee paused. Mary Scarlett was a Blakely. Why hadn't she put that together on the boat? But why would Mary Scarlett's kin say that she was to marry her brother? It made no sense.

Mary Scarlett's face shut down, blank of all expression. The silence between them lasted long enough for the afternoon shadows to lengthen on the polished wood floor. Mary Scarlett held onto the bright green and yellow quilt top, sliding a thumb back and forth over it until Viola Lee feared she would rub a hole in it.

The grandfather clock in the hallway groaned and chimed out the hour. Seven gongs.

Viola Lee waited for Mary Scarlett to explain, to take the fear away.

"You know something, don't you?" Viola Lee said. When Mary Scarlett did not respond, she tried again. "Is he kin to you, this man?"

"I don't want to talk about it any further," Mary Scarlett jabbed a pin into the quilt. "Foolish people say foolish things."

Anger rose in Viola Lee, a cold, hard thing. It lodged in her chest, surprising her with its weight. Her arms felt heavy, her legs weak. What dreadful secret was Mary Scarlett hiding?

Was there some truth in what the man said? Was James her brother? If so, had James figured it out? Was that why he had disappeared?

The door opened and John Sebring walked in with his usual jaunty gait. He whistled as he hung his hat on the hat rack and set his cane in the umbrella stand. It clanked and rattled.

"Ahh," he said, his smile jolly, "my two beauties. What a pleasure coming home to you."

The sweet sincerity of his words nearly broke Viola Lee's heart.

He stopped and looked from Viola Lee's face to Mary Scarlett's.

"Hello, Daddy!" Viola Lee said, and hugged him hard, drinking in the clean smell of the starch in his shirt. Maybe her daddy could soothe the fear that had just grabbed hold of her soul, tell her there was nothing to worry about, that it would all be fine.

He kissed her cheek and held his arms out to Mary Scarlett.

Mary Scarlett's gaze was withering. "So, did you manage to bring home anything other than your appetite?"

Viola Lee felt a sudden surge of guilt at the relief she felt when her mother's anger turned from herself to her father.

She wanted desperately to hear something lighthearted and gay, something that would turn the clock back to before the horrible thought filled her with such fear. "Where did you drive today, Daddy?"

The flush on her father's face told her that question would not bring about the desired results.

"Did you pick up your clients and deliver them safely to their destination in time for them to catch the ferry?" Mary Scarlett asked after his momentary pause and the sudden droop of his shoulders.

Her father sighed and shook his head. "No," he said, shame on his face. But abruptly, as if remembering something that gave him strength, he straightened his shoulders and grinned. "I got held up on my way in town by a big old gator sunning himself in the middle of the road. Biggest gator I ever saw. Must have been twelve feet long and three feet thick," he nodded with the assurance of someone confident in a sympathetic audience.

"Twelve feet, huh?" Mary Scarlett shook her head. "You and your tall tales." She surveyed the quilt layers, snatched up more pins, and stabbed the fabric, punctuating her words with each stab. "You wait to the last minute to do everything," stab, stab, "you should have started earlier," stab, stab. "Smart people build in time for possible delays. Fools don't. Do you ever think ahead?" she asked. "No," she answered herself, studying the neatly pinned quilt top. "How I've lived with you this long is beyond me."

Viola Lee backed quietly out of the room, disappointed that her father hadn't been able to cheer Mary Scarlett, but, in a strange sort of way, relieved that Mary Scarlett had started in on her age-old ramble about her father's shortcomings. It was almost soothing, Mary Scarlett's version of a lullaby, the sting cancelled out by familiarity.

Her father stood at the sideboard. Having tuned her mother out, he unfolded the day's paper and murmured agreeably, "You are right, Mary Scarlett."

She snatched up the quilt, hauled it over to her Singer, and continued the rampage.

In the quiet coolness of her bedroom, a crisp white sheet peeking out from behind the lacey, intricately crocheted bedspread—Mary Scarlett's handiwork—Viola Lee mulled over the events of the day.

Viola Lee remembered his red-veined face, Annie Laura's firm stance, and the man backing away.

But he had returned for the final blow. Blakely said her mother traded her for a piece of land.

Had her mother truly abandoned her? Had she traded her for land, signing papers that gave up her rights to Viola Lee?

Had Annie Laura been a whore? Why did he say she was marrying her brother?

And to whom could Viola Lee go for the truth?

❧

Late in the night, Viola Lee was awakened by the sounds of a heated argument between John Sebring and Mary Scarlett. Arguments between them were not unusual. But the normal cadence was Mary Scarlett's angry accusations buffered by John Sebring's placid, conversational responses. Tonight was different. It was John Sebring who was angry, and the anger in his voice was beyond anything Viola Lee had ever heard from her happy, easygoing father.

"I told you never to allow that man in my house," John Sebring said.

"He's my brother. What am I supposed to do? Stand at the door with a shotgun and keep him from entering?"

"Yes," John Sebring said. "And that's exactly what I'll do if he ever sets foot on this property again."

Her normally combative mother was silent.

"What has he ever done but bring you heartache and pain?" John Sebring asked.

"You don't understand," Mary Scarlett said. "What happened to him scarred him."

"And God made you to fix him?" John Sebring asked. "Don't you understand that some things can't be fixed?"

"People can," Mary Scarlett said, her voice breaking. "I'll never give up hope that one day, Walter Blakely's troubled mind will be healed. He has to have someone who believes in him, John. Don't you understand? If everyone gives up hope in him, what has he to live for?"

"Oh, girl," John Sebring said softly. "Don't you know that God is the only one who can heal people? And don't you know that a person has to want to be healed before any change can happen? You have got to drop that burden. If Walter heals or doesn't, it's not on you. Did you ever think that the fact that he knows you are always there to fix his problems might be what is standing in the way of him fixing himself?"

"It's too late now anyway," Mary Scarlett said. "He'll go to prison for sure for what he's done. But if you knew what he was like before, it would pain you like it pains me. He was such a sweet little boy, so eager to help Mama, so full of love for her."

"I know this is hard for you to hear, but a lot of people live through horrible tragedies and come out okay. In pain, but okay. Walter didn't come out okay. He came out angry and filled with hate, willing to take his anger out on any poor woman who he perceived questioned his power. Only God can work the miracle that will change Walter Blakely. You are helpless. Leave it alone. Do not send him any more lawyer money."

They must have grown quiet after that. Viola Lee slipped back into a troubled sleep.

Chapter 4

Annie Laura braided her hair and looked out the window over the vast acreage she had fought so hard to keep. A pain rose in her chest like a sob, a fat ball of anger and heartache that she could not afford to allow out. She had made the right choice all of those years ago, hadn't she? She wound the braid into a tight bun. She had given Viola Lee a better life, a life she herself could not possibly have afforded.

She stopped pinning her bun for just a moment, held it in place with one hand, and looked at herself in the bedroom mirror. Had she made the decision to save Viola Lee, or herself?

Yesterday, she had traveled to Grassy Glade to meet her daughter and confess. She had hoped that her daughter would forgive her and would understand why she did what she did.

But the trust she saw in that child's blue eyes when she first called her "Mama" stopped Annie Laura cold. She knew she hadn't the courage to break her child's heart any more than it had already been broken. The past was best left in the past. No one could understand the gut-wrenching decision she had been forced to make. No one.

She wouldn't let herself think about the man on the ferry. Had Viola Lee heard him? *Did you tell her you traded her for a piece of land?* Viola Lee acted as though she had not heard. Annie Laura feared she had. She pressed the hairpins into her bun. The past was the past. All she had was the present. She plopped her Sunday hat on her head. And she planned to make the best of it.

Today she would figure out how best to help Viola Lee and her fiancé, James. She was a coward with a purpose.

The pre-dawn sky rumbled with the threat of an early spring storm. She had work to do before she could leave the farm again. Annie Laura studied the mottled pink and gray clouds, gauging the possibility of a storm interfering with her plans to break the Sabbath and ready the north field for planting. She consoled herself with the thought that even Jesus sometimes found it necessary to work on the Sabbath.

And, like Jesus, she was single. Or nearly so. The sweet man she had married was not the man she lived with now. He had changed, and Annie Laura tried not to hate him for it. Some days it was easier than others. Today was one of the hard days.

She gathered her wiggling brood, piled them in the wagon, headed to church, paid her tithe, prayed, and gave thanks to the God who made her whole. After service, she fed her children their Sunday dinner—ham, the last of the green beans she'd canned this past summer, and hoecake.

Lord, but it had grown hot. While they sat around the table sharing Sunday school antics, she rose from the table, walked into her tiny bedroom, stepped out of her wool serge skirt and crisply ironed, ruffled blouse, hung them neatly on a nail to air out, donned her overalls, hat and gloves, and headed toward the door.

She felt her children's eyes on her, and she consoled them. "Don't worry, your mama hasn't gone crazy. You all enjoy the afternoon, but clean that table off first and lay the food in the pie safe. Go on, now, I got things to do."

She was met with silence. She walked outside into the oppressive pre-storm heat. When she hitched the mule, she heard gleeful laughter and general rejoicing. The children were thrilled to pieces that she wasn't asking them to plow the fields on a Sunday, their only day of rest. Annie Laura set to plowing alone.

The plow jumped and skipped in the root-bound soil. It had been many years since she'd cleared the pines and oaks from the land, but they left their reminders still, as if life was precious, too precious to be forgotten. *Remember us,* they whispered, *remember.* And she did, every time the plow balked and skittered. She forced a straight, clean line in the rich earth in hopes that next year, on this field at least, she would be able to forget. She resented the land as much as she loved it. The land had brought her security and food and clothing for her children, but it had taken away her Viola Lee.

Sweat trickled down her back and chest, and dirt from the plow spewed into her eyes when she hit another root. She cried black tears. She paused for a moment to wipe her eyes and looked ahead. The vision before her was overwhelming—she would have to plow into the night to finish. The sky rumbled. She mopped her face again with the kerchief she kept tied around her neck. Heat like this was unusual for a day in April. It felt more like a September storm brewing, though the sun shone and the air was still.

She comforted herself by looking back at what she had already accomplished. The neat furrows made her heart sing. She grasped the plow tight, the handles familiar, the wood worn to the shape of her hands. Her husband, Leonard, wasn't made to be a farmer. But she was. She'd settled two farms in her thirty and some years. She'd tamed the land, urged life from sandy soil, forced it to grow corn, cotton, and sweet potatoes. She knew what grew best, when, and where. Eager to learn all she could about successful farming, she'd spent many hours at the feed store pretending to shop; in truth, she lingered to listen as the farmers swapped their stories.

For a girl born and raised in Germany for the first fifteen years of her life, she made a respectable Florida Cracker. She raised the skinny Florida sheep and cows, she managed a henhouse whose hens produced smooth brown eggs, and she grew enough vegetables to keep her family healthy, with some leftover to sell at the roadside stand or Mr. Tiller's store, whichever one brought her the most profit. She'd done well in spite of the odds stacked against her.

"Mama!" The sound of Louise's voice broke her reverie.

"Whoa," Annie Laura said to the mule, and shaded her eyes in the harsh afternoon sun. She waited until her sweet daughter reached her. Louise was a pretty girl. She had not inherited her father's height, which might be a blessing. Her hair shone golden brown in the sun. She traipsed across the newly plowed field, careful to avoid the neat furrows.

"Mama, I've come to help you, and don't you say no. You can't make me go away." Her serious, pecan-shaped eyes wide, she continued, "Jessie's keeping an eye on the others, and promises to run out here and tell if they're getting into any mischief. Now you just tell me what you want me to do, and I'm going to do it."

Annie's heart swelled with the kindness of Louise's words. "I reckon I know you well enough to know that nothing I say is going to change your mind."

Louise laughed a relieved laugh. "Thank you, Mama," she said.

Annie Laura shook her head. This daughter thanked her for letting her work the land until her hands were blistered and her face burnt by the fierce sun.

"You're a sweet girl, Louise," Annie Laura said.

"No, Mama," Louise said, her words fierce, "I'm not sweet. If I were sweet, I wouldn't stay so angry at Daddy all the time."

Annie Laura sucked in her breath. What was it this time? *Please, Lord,* she prayed, *don't let me have to go pick him up and pay a fine today. I've got too much to do.* She took a deep breath to steady herself. "Why are you angry with your father?" she asked.

"The same reason as always. Why is it that you have to do all the work? Daddy ain't nothin' but a drunken lout." Louise clenched her fists.

Rage flashed through Annie, though she wasn't certain who she was most angry at. Leonard for causing Louise such pain, or herself for allowing it to happen. "Don't you speak like that against your daddy. You apologize right this minute."

Louise looked away from Annie, studied the ground, but Annie Laura could feel Louise's anger. Fury was her only defense. Louise saw Leonard for what he was: a drunken dreamer who wasted the hard-earned family money on corn liquor and jail fines.

"Why isn't he out here helping you?" Louise asked through gritted teeth.

"He's fishing," Annie Laura said. "And when he comes home and sells the fish, we'll be able to buy more seeds to plant this field with."

Louise looked up at her mama and shook her head and smiled. "When was the last time you depended on Daddy for money to plant the fields? You've got money socked away for seeding and planting like you always do, and whatever Daddy brings home—if he brings anything—you put in his own money pot that probably goes to pay his jail fines."

Annie Laura had to swallow a laugh at her daughter's acuity. She was right.

"You been spying?" she asked, but her words were kind, and Louise smiled.

"You go on ahead of me," Annie Laura said, pointing to the sandy earth in front of the plow. "You check for stones and move them when you see them, and warn me if you see any big roots. They slither in like snakes every spring."

Louise nodded, tied on her bonnet, and scampered ahead of the mule, stopping first to pat her soft side.

Annie Laura had fallen in love with Leonard when they were both young and hurting and could only see the young and hurting in each other. He'd looked at her with those big brown eyes, and she knew that he understood her pain because he'd had plenty of his own. Illegitimate child of a Creek Indian daddy and an unmarried mama, he knew what it felt like to be scorned. It was like that with people who'd known pain growing up. Put them all in a room with folks who'd had it easy, and they'd find each other.

Leonard had taken care of her. He'd nursed her through her anger and pain at losing Viola Lee and had given her a baby of her own they could keep. When the babies kept on coming, Leonard resented them and took to drinking. Maybe she should have been more understanding. But she hadn't. And now the ugly was all that was left of the sweet, tender boy she'd married.

Truth was, she could fix her fields and fix her kids. She could fix food and fix a sore. But she couldn't fix her marriage.

The air was still, too still, and the heat surrounded Annie, pressing her down. She plowed on ahead, the mule ambling along, the "shh, shh, shh" of the plow in the earth a steady song, soothing in its repetition.

Without warning, the hair stood up on Annie's arms and the back of her neck. In an instant, she knew what was coming. She dropped the plow and screamed, "Louise! Lightning coming, get down!" She looked for Louise, couldn't see her. "Louise!" she screamed, but before she could find her child, a flash of light, and pain unlike any she had ever experienced, wracked her body. Annie

Laura fell, a deafening boom rattled the ground, and the world went black.

৵

"Mama!" Louise's voice sounded weak like it came from under water.

She looked up into a sky that was disturbingly blue. A hand reached down from it. Was it God? Annie Laura squeezed her eyes shut, opened them again, and recognized the hand as Louise's.

Annie Laura tried to reach for her daughter's hand, gave it all she had, but her arm wouldn't move, nor her legs nor her hands nor feet. *No, Lord,* Annie Laura prayed, *I got too much to do. I can't be lying around in this dirt.*

"Mama!" Louise said. Her voice was clear, and it sounded like she was right down there beside Annie. She felt water dripping on her face and thought it was rain, but no, when she opened her eyes and looked up, it was tears dripping from Louise's face.

"Come on, Mama," Louise said. "We got to get inside before the rain. Lightning flashing everywhere, and you and me got to get back to the house. Please, Mama." Her voice broke, and her soft hands touched Annie's face, hands that reminded Annie Laura of her own mama caressing her as if she were a child. She rested under the caress for a moment, felt herself falling into a dark, deep blackness where her heart didn't ache so bad.

And then she remembered the mule.

Annie bolted upright and looked around her. "*Wo ist das Maultier?*" she asked. "*Das Maultier?*" she repeated, her voice urgent.

"Oh, Mama!" Louise said, delight wrinkling a smile at the corner of her eyes. "You're alive. I thought you dead for sure."

"*Wo ist das Maultier?*" Annie Laura asked, and scrambled to her feet.

Louise looked at her wide-eyed. "I don't know what you are saying, Mama. You're talking gibberish."

Annie Laura looked at Louise. What was the matter with her child? Why didn't she understand her? She asked again.

This time, realization dawned in Louise's eyes. "Why, Dolly's over there, taking shelter under that tree," she said and pointed to a loblolly pine so tall that it seemed to reach to heaven.

"*Wir müssen sie zu bekommen. Lightning wird durch dieses Kiefern anbraten und braten Sie sie für das Abendessen. Beeilung!*" Annie Laura ran, but her vision was blurry, and running straight took everything she had. Dolly had to be gotten inside. The farm would go under without that mule.

She reached the mule just as the rain began, pelting them like a volley of clay balls shot from the end of a sky full of Daisy air rifles the rich little town boys kept. She felt Louise's feet pounding the ground behind her.

Her vision was fuzzy and the mule wobbled. She grabbed at the mule. She missed the halter, and Louise grabbed it for her. "*Gib es mir!*" Annie Laura said.

Louise looked at Annie Laura with frightened eyes. "Mama, I don't know what you are saying."

Annie Laura snatched the worn leather strapping from Louise's hand. Why couldn't her child understand her?

"Dolly will only come with me when she's scared," Annie Laura said.

Tears sparkled in the corners of Louise's eyes, but she handed the worn leather strapping over.

Rain fell in torrents; soon, the field would be a muddy clay pit.

"Get up, girl," Annie Laura hollered at the mule, her voice guttural. "*Kommen Sie, bevor Sie getötet.*"

The mule obliged, and the three sloshed through the clay and mud, through the pelting rain towards the barn. Lightning flashed again. Annie Laura moaned, grabbed Louise's hand with her free one, and they sprinted the last few yards. The mule understood and trotted behind as quickly as her four stubby legs could carry her.

They settled the mule, sprinted to the house, and peeled off their sodden clothes.

"Mama!" Louise said, horrified. "What's that all over your chest and arms?"

"*Was?*" Annie Laura responded.

"It's all over you like someone took a thin red crayon and drew a lightning strike all over your chest and down your arms. What is that?"

Annie Laura picked up her hand mirror and studied the lines all over her chest. Louise was right, it looked like an artist had used her chest and arms for a canvas to draw a lightning strike in red. She'd heard of such from farmers talking in the general store, but had never seen it herself. She also knew it would fade in a few days.

"*Mach dir keine Sorgen,*" Annie Laura said. "*Es wird sich in ein paar Tagen.*"

"Why is Mama speaking German? And what is that on her neck?" Jessie traced the red line with a tentative, gentle hand.

"Oh!" Louise said. "I thought she was talking gibberish. I don't know. She got struck by lightning."

"Lightning?" Jessie said. "Oh, Mama!" He wrapped his arms around Annie, and Annie Laura pulled away.

"*Mir geht es gut, keine Sorge,*" Mama said. The pain radiated all over her body.

"She says it will go away soon, not to worry. She could have been killed. It's a miracle she isn't. She needs to go to bed."

"I don't think Mama is inclined to go to bed right here in the middle of the day," Louise responded.

Why were they speaking to her as if she wasn't there? And German? She had reverted to her native language without realizing it. No wonder Louise couldn't understand her. And she was thankful for Jessie's insistence on learning German. She'd not wanted to teach him; she had wanted her child to be completely American, unlike Annie Laura herself. But Jessie had insisted. He said he wanted to be able to read Annie Laura's German Bible, the one that had belonged to her own mother, and he wanted to be able to read the diary left by Annie's father, the grandfather he had never known. Jessie, always the sensitive one, said that learning German helped the dead come alive for him. And how could Annie Laura argue with keeping her parents alive?

Annie Laura thought she felt her mother's hands on her, stroking her forehead gently. She tried to sleep, but the question burned in her as if the lightning had set it afire. Was it possible that the man who raped her had also fathered James?

What if she could find Viola Lee's fiancé and prove that he was not her brother, regardless of what town gossip held to be true?

According to Viola Lee, James was a logger, deep in the woods of south Alabama, just over the Florida line. Annie Laura could probably get the camp's exact location from the postmaster over in Waterfall.

She ticked off the days on her finger. Today was Sunday; the wedding was Saturday. That didn't leave her much time to work with, and she had a lot to settle here on her farm before she could just haul off and leave.

Annie Laura needed to find James. She had to find out who his daddy was. She couldn't let her baby girl marry her own brother.

Good Friday came at the end of this week, and the fields had to be planted before then. If she got it done today and tomorrow, that would leave her a day or two to find James. She considered leaving the young'uns with Louise in charge. She'd never left them overnight—just those twice a year day visits to Grassy Glade.

She knew what she had to do, saw it with startling clarity. She had to make things right with Leonard, and James and Viola Lee. She would not abide Leonard's foolishness any longer. And she needed to go find James. But first, she must sleep. The lightning striking her might have been the best thing that ever happened. Just after the lighting struck, she'd seen a vision—several, really. Each like a picture, floating all around her head. Leonard and James and Viola Lee had arranged themselves so that she knew what she need-ed to do. But there was another picture that she couldn't figure out. Viola Lee screaming and a well nearby.

Chapter 5

Annie Laura awoke with a start when she heard her youngest crying. The rain played a steady rat-a-tat-tat against the tin roof.

"I want to play, too!"

"Well, stop throwing the cards on the floor, and we'll let you," Louise replied. "Now straighten up. You're going to wake Mama."

"I don't care! You can't make me stop playing. Only Mama can tell me what to do."

Annie Laura dressed hurriedly and stepped out into the kitchen. "What is all of this about?"

"Mama!" the children shouted. "You're alive!" they said, and clambered around to hug her.

"Did the lightning stay right on you like Jessie said?"

"I want to see."

"Come on, now," Louise said, pulling them away.

"It's all right, Louise," Annie Laura said. "I'm much better now. The pain seems to have subsided. I just feel a little stiff and maybe a little dizzy. Where's your daddy?" she asked, hugging her smallest child, John Wesley, who was three, and touching Jessie's cheeks.

"He ain't home yet, Mama," Louise replied with big eyes.

Silence fell on the room. And fear, oppressive, like the air before the storm, snaked its way from child to child. Louise clutched her skirt, squeezed it until her knuckles were white. She moved away from her siblings and uncovered the sewing machine. The wooden cover banged against the wood floor. They jumped at the sound like they'd been scalded. She put a voluminous skirt on the machine and began sewing a side seam, cranking the machine as fast as she could.

John Wesley slid his hand into his big brother's, and Jessie gripped it.

Scared of their own daddy. That wasn't how it was supposed to be. This had gone on for far too long. Something had to change.

"What was all that noise about I heard earlier?" she asked. "What happened while I was sleeping to cause such a fuss?"

Her words had their intended effect, and the atmosphere in the room changed immediately from fear to exuberant storytelling.

The younger children all began to talk at once, each with a story of what happened in the card game.

John Wesley stuck his bottom lip out. "Louise said I couldn't play anymore."

Louise stopped her furious sewing to listen.

"Well," Annie Laura said. "And did you throw the cards on the floor?"

"They weren't playing right," Jessie piped up. He loosened his hand from John Wesley's and gestured with both hands. "They made him lose every time."

Jessie's sense of what was right and what was wrong was strong. So strong that he found himself defending the weak, who, more often than not, lost interest in the battle while Jessie continued fighting for their rights.

"You want to come out here and help me? I've got some work to do in the field. It's going to be dark soon, and I need someone to hold my lantern."

"I will, let me!" The other children jumped up and down at the chance to help her.

Jessie squared his shoulders. "Which lantern do you want me to use?"

Annie Laura smiled. "The big red one out in the barn," she said. "Go on, now. Get it for me, and hurry back."

His face was a study in seriousness as he set out on his mission. But first, he turned to Louise.

"Y'all be nice to John Wesley, you hear me?"

Louise nodded. "I'll make sure of it."

❧

Leonard's two-day bender meant they'd probably all have to spend the night under the old oak tree, deep in the back of the sloping yard. The tree grew behind the henhouse and behind the barn, but close enough to Aunt Martha's house to go get the help of her shotgun if need be.

Annie Laura prayed Leonard would wait until after she'd finished the plowing to get home. Tomorrow was the only day she could spare to go find James. She had to oversee the planting come Tuesday. It was Good Friday week and she wasn't sure how long it would take to plant all the fields. The work was long, hard, and relentless. She wondered if it would ever end. Would there be a day when she could take a rest from the root rot in the north field and bugs and varmints in the south?

"Mama, you slept right through the storm," Louise said, opening the door for Annie. "It like to have taken away the house."

"And things blew all over the yard. It's going to take all of us to pick everything up," Jessie said holding the lantern. "You reckon this rain's going to stop soon?"

"Probably, but a little rain never hurt anybody," Annie Laura smiled. "What are we waiting for?"

"In the rain?"

"In the rain," Annie Laura answered, and tousled his soft, brown hair. The lightning and thunder were far away, no longer posing any danger, and she knew the children would enjoy the exertion.

They filed out of the door and down the stairs, her grown babies, old enough to help out now, all of them.

If they started now, maybe it would all be picked up before Leonard got home. The fewer excuses he had for getting riled up and taking it out on the children, the better. Of course lately he hadn't needed excuses. She had to stop dwelling on the bad side of Leonard, had to find the bright side that would help her carry on, but it was getting harder. She wondered if it was this baby? Pregnancy sometimes wore on her like that, making her sadness more pronounced. She would have to shake it off like she had so many times before.

"Mama, are you really going to plow through the night?" Louise asked.

"I'll have to check the fields in the remaining light to see if the rain made a river or watered the soil." She prayed that the soil had drained off well enough to be able to plow.

"Mama, you going to plant butterbeans?" Jessie asked.

"Yes, son, I am. That and a few other vegetables," she said.

There was a collective groan.

"But, Mama, if you plant butterbeans, we have to get on our knees to pick them all."

"And then, we got to shell all those things. That takes a long time, Mama. Can't you just plant you some snap beans?"

"A little time on your knees never hurt anybody," she said. "You can use it to thank the good Lord for land that belongs to us. Aren't you glad you're not a sharecropper, having to give all your first fruits to some landowner who never does a lick of work? We're blessed, and you be sure to take time to give thanks for it."

"Now, get to cleaning," she said.

The children whooped and hollered as they made a game of picking up in the rain. "I'm gonna get the most, Mama," John Wesley boasted.

Annie Laura smiled. "I look forward to seeing it," she said. She called Louise over to her. "You come get me if you see your daddy coming in, you hear me? You make sure you do your cleaning down by the road so you'll have plenty of time to send someone after me."

Louise gritted her teeth, lifted her chin high. "I hate—"

"Now," Annie Laura put her finger over Louise's lips, "don't you say something you'll live to regret."

Louise pressed her lips tightly together, nodded, and turned to walk down the wheel-rutted clay drive leading to the main road.

Annie Laura felt her daughter's pain; her heart contracted with it. She remembered too well her own daddy before he'd quit drinking, his rages, her own fear. And here she had created the same cycle all over again.

That was going to end tonight.

Jessie gestured to the lantern. "Mama, is this the one you wanted?" he asked solemnly.

"Yes, son. This is exactly the right one. Now let's check to make sure there is plenty of kerosene, and you get an old rag to hold it with. You want to protect your hand when that metal gets too hot to hold."

"Yes, ma'am. I'll do it. Can I light it now?"

"Not yet. Sun's still in the sky, though it's hiding behind the clouds. I need to check out the fields. Do you want to go with me?"

"Yes, ma'am. I'll help make sure you don't trip out there, Mama. And I'll be on the lookout for lightning."

Trip? She wondered why he was worried about her tripping. She strode out to the plowing she'd done earlier and realized her gait was off, that she was walking crooked. Had the lightning strike damaged her balance? The plow would steady her, but what would keep her from making crooked lines? Dolly, her faithful mule, would go where she guided her.

"Can you walk a straight line?" she asked Jessie.

"Yes, ma'am," he said, his face serious. "I can."

"Well, then," she said, "I'm going to have to rely on you. Looks like this lightning *has* made me walk funny. I need you to walk ahead of Dolly when we plow. You make sure the rows are plowed straight."

"You can depend on me, Mama," Jessie said. "I'll make sure they are straight."

The child was so eager to please, it hurt her heart.

He placed the lantern carefully at the edge of the field for when it got dark, and took Annie's hand in his small, warm one. After eating a hurried dinner of cold biscuits stuffed with ham, they began plowing the field, Jessie leading her straight.

The rain stopped, but darkness fell anyway, and Annie Laura sent Jessie back for the lantern. She used a pine branch to mark the place she'd left off plowing.

She waited to see the light of his lantern. Soon the light flared and glowed, and she began her wobbly trek to the south side of the field to meet her child. She hoped her lightning-induced vertigo would clear up by tomorrow.

"Mama!" Louise's warning cry pierced the evening sky. Leonard was home. Annie Laura picked up her skirts and ran as best she could. She had to get to Jessie before Leonard did. She tripped and fell, her mouth tasted mud, and she pulled herself up and ran again. The flare was moving toward her steadily. Suddenly, the flare jerked, stood high, and then flew through the air like fourth-of-July fireworks. It landed on the ground, and fire spread across the field, following the path of the fresh kerosene. Annie Laura ran.

She heard Jessie scream, and heard Leonard's laughter.

"What you scared of, you old crybaby?" Leonard yelled.

He didn't see Annie Laura coming. He held Jessie high in the air, above the kerosene flames.

Annie Laura felt a burst of anger unlike any she had felt before. This was not going to happen again. Leonard would not terrorize her babies. Ever again. A surge of energy coursed through her and she ran. She ran through the flames and, with the full force of her body, pushed Leonard.

Leonard hit the ground, Jessie with him. "Mama!" Jessie cried.

"Let him go," Annie Laura's words came out harsh and stone wall solid.

In his surprise, Leonard did just as she said.

"Go, Jessie," she said. "Find Louise." Jessie hurtled away.

Leonard regained his composure, grabbed her thin arm in his iron fist, twisted it behind her. "You trying to take my son away from me?" he asked, breathing out the foul smell of stale whiskey. He licked his lips and pulled her towards him. "You always have been a purty little thing when you're angry. How about a little kiss for your husband?" he said.

Annie Laura averted her face, and the kiss landed squarely on her ear, the slurping sound sickening.

She'd loved this man once, before the drink had turned him sour. Now, she abided him. She took her marriage vow seriously, and would not part with him until death. Which she hoped, God forgive her, would come soon.

"Don't," Annie Laura said. "Ever."

"Ever, huh?" Leonard said. "What is it? You getting it from somewhere else? Is that it?"

"You're not the man I married," Annie Laura said. She didn't know why she was even bothering to talk to him. He was drunk and out of his head.

Suddenly he fixed her with eyes that looked in the firelight to be sober. "You went down and saw her again, didn't you? Is that what this is about? You don't think you need me—you don't need us anymore? Is that one pathetic child down in Grassy Glade your new family? You made a promise to me," he said. "You promised me that you would forget that child, that we would start our own family, that you would never look back, only forward. But every year, twice a year, you look back. What are you trying to recapture, Annie Laura? Whatever it is, you'll never find it down there."

Tears, sudden and unbidden, rose in Annie Laura's eyes and choked the sense out of her. She spat in his face.

"So that's how it is," he said, his words slurring. She could imagine his red eyes, halfway closed. Darkness spared her that. He yanked her to him, and she cried out at the painful crush of his hands.

"Lick it off," he said, forcing her mouth to the wet slime on his face. She kicked his shin. He jerked back, let go of her arm, and she ran, stumbling back to the house. "I'm coming after you," he said. "Don't think I won't. I know where you're going." He worked himself up into a rage, and she feared the monster she had created.

She did not hear the children, but she didn't expect to. They were carefully silent. They knew the drill. Louise would have gathered them all and led them quietly down the backyard hill, and Louise would have gotten the quilt and anything else she had time to grab.

Annie Laura wondered when he would figure out their hiding place. So far, he passed out before finding them. She could only pray that this would be another of those nights.

The darkness hid her, and she ran her wobbly course to the back of the house, down the sloping yard, past the henhouse, past the barn, until she reached the sheltering oak. She ran by memory, for the night was a black, moonless one, the clouds still heavy. She prayed the rain had stopped for good. She feared it had not.

She reached the children, huddled around the giant oak.

"I've got a quilt like you said, Mama," Mary whispered. "But it's too wet to put down."

"You did good," Mama said. Her children gathered around her and clutched her skirts, huddling close for her protection. Louise held John Wesley in her arms. He reached for Annie Laura, and she took him. She held the child against her, swaying a little to calm him. She squeezed her eyes together, opening and shutting them, willing away the vertigo. The night could be long, and she needed all of her senses alert.

A whispering breeze blew through the oak, rattled the wet leaves, raining their excess upon her and her children. The children shook off the water, but as the temperature dropped, they shivered.

"Mama, we're going to freeze to death out here," Louise said.

A kerosene lantern glowed in the back window of the house. They heard the crashing rage of their daddy. Annie Laura felt Jessie tense up, and Annie Laura knew they prayed the same prayer. *Please, Lord, don't let him get the sewing machine.*

The rattling grew more intense, and they could hear the crashing of crockery in the cool, damp night. They heard him roar, "Annie! What have you done with my babies? You've taken them, all of them. I only want to see my babies. ANNIE!!! I'm going to kill you, woman, when I get my hands on you. Where are my babies?"

John Wesley, whimpered. "Don't let him kill you, Mama," his voice choked with tears.

"Don't you worry," Jessie whispered, and Annie Laura could hear the thrust of his chin in his voice. "I'll protect her." He spread himself in front of Annie, stretched his nine- year-old arms across all of them as if he were a fence, and dared his father to try coming through.

Louise shivered. "Mama, we can't stay out here much longer. You want me to go down and see if Aunt Martha's awake?"

"Not yet," Annie Laura said. "Maybe he'll go on to sleep, pass out, and we can sleep in our own beds tonight." She hated imposing on Martha, and getting all the children bedded down in a strange house was difficult at best. More importantly, she feared what Martha would do when she found Leonard had threatened Annie Laura and the children again. Annie Laura prayed Leonard would tire soon.

But the crashing went on, Leonard bellowing like a bull trapped in a barn. He raged against the sun and the moon, and cursed Annie Laura to the stars.

When the temperature continued to drop, and the children, even Louise and Mary, shivered from cold more than fear, Annie Laura knew she would have to take them to Aunt Martha's.

"Quiet, now," she told them. "We're going to go see if Aunt Martha's got any sweet potatoes cooked for us this cold night."

"You reckon Aunt Martha's going to kill him this time?" Louise whispered into Annie's ear.

"I hope not," Annie Laura lied.

The children followed her as quietly as they could through the dark of the night.

Annie Laura took a deep breath and herded her children to Aunt Martha's cozy cabin, the one with the loaded shotgun perched just inside the door.

Chapter 6

The smell of roasting sweet potatoes filled the night air, leading Annie Laura and her bedraggled children to Aunt Martha's cabin. Annie Laura took a deep breath and called out, "It's me, Annie."

Aunt Martha's loaded shotgun made it necessary to identify herself before crossing the front porch. The door opened, just a crack, and the cabin, enveloped in darkness, kept its secrets.

"Why, Annie Laura," Aunt Martha said, the corncob pipe dangling from her lips. "Come on in. And it looks like you've brought me some company. Come on, children. Give your Aunt Martha a kiss," she growled, teasing the children. She either had a corncob pipe dangling, and with it the stale smell of tobacco smoke, or worse, a mouthful of snuff, which she dipped from a shiny container the size of a silver dollar. Her polished silver spittoon sat on the floor beside the fireplace. Sometimes, a little stray spittle dribbled down her chin. The children grew wide-eyed when they were forced to kiss her, and this delighted the old woman. Her laughter cackled through the cabin.

After the necessary ceremony, Aunt Martha settled the children around the fireplace and doled out roasted sweet potatoes, which she slathered with brown sugar, cinnamon, and a generous dollop of butter. She served the fare in tin plates and handed each child a wooden spoon. "You help your little brother," she said to Jessie.

"Yes, ma'am," Jessie said, pleased with the responsibility.

"Where's Grandma?" Louise asked.

"She's out delivering a baby," Aunt Martha said. "She said she wouldn't be back until tomorrow."

Louise's face fell. She was a special favorite of her grandmother, Mary, her daddy's mama.

Aunt Martha patted her shoulder. "I'll tell her you asked about her."

Louise smiled and nodded.

Annie Laura was almost relieved that her mother-in-law, Mary, was out delivering a baby. Even though Annie Laura knew Mary loved her, and pitied her for having to put up with Leonard, telling his mother her son was drunk again and scaring his own children was hard.

Once the children were settled, Aunt Martha pulled Annie Laura out onto the front porch. "I don't reckon this is a social call," she said, "not this long after dark on a rainy night."

"No, ma'am," Annie Laura said, and wondered if she had made a mistake. Maybe even now Leonard had calmed down and the house would be normal, and she could pretend, as she had for years, that everything was going to be alright. The thought didn't hold any power over her.

Life was easier when Leonard was gone, and Annie Laura applauded him for "going fishing." But wasn't that true for most husbands? She'd heard other wives talking about their relief when their husbands were gone for a day or two. Was Leonard so different from other husbands? This was the same conversation she'd had with herself for years, but tonight, she knew it was a lie. Leonard was not like other husbands. He was a drunk.

When Leonard came back without any fish, she pretended it had just been a bad day for fishing and said nothing. To speak of it would bring his wrath upon them all.

Aunt Martha pulled her shotgun off the gun rack over her front door and took her place on the rickety rocking chair. She settled in and leaned back, the rocker squeaking and moaning. The only thing shining in the dark, moonless night was the barrel of her gun. It glinted in the light reflected from the single kerosene lantern.

Annie Laura craned her neck to check on the children through the side window. She could see them happily eating sweet potatoes, licking their fingers for the satisfying buttery cinnamon.

"They're fine," Aunt Martha said, following her glance.

"I don't know about that," Annie Laura said. She took a deep breath, found she couldn't talk, found that the woman of action she had been for the last few hours was gone, and what was left was a trembling shell.

"What's wrong with you?" Aunt Martha said. "You don't seem right. You carrying again?"

Annie Laura ignored the last question and answered the first.

"I got struck by lightning this afternoon."

"Did you learn anything?" Aunt Martha asked, her bright eyes searching. She leaned into Annie's face, peered into her eyes, and the smell of pipe tobacco was fresh and sweet.

"Go ahead and light your pipe if you want to," Annie Laura said, pulling away from the older woman's scrutiny. "I reckon we interrupted you."

"No," Aunt Martha said. "I enjoy the smell of fresh tobacco. Sometimes I carry it around all night before lighting it. What did you see that scared you?"

"Nothing," Annie Laura said. But that was a lie. Startled, she remembered that in the brief moment after the lightning flash, she'd understood everything. Life had spread out before her like a neat canvas, and she knew exactly what it was she needed to do. Keep Viola Lee away from Blakely. He meant her harm. Find James. And something about her marriage. Leonard had come to her in that vision, innocent and clean, before the drinking, begging her to find him again. But Leonard wasn't lost. He was right here.

"What?" Aunt Martha pushed. "You had a vision?"

"Viola Lee is in danger."

"Danger? From where?"

"Walter Blakely."

"I thought he was up in Dothan awaiting trial for raping that poor girl," Aunt Martha responded and stuffed a thimbleful of tobacco into her pipe.

"I saw him yesterday in St. Andrews. He's out on bail."

Aunt Martha pushed the tobacco down in her pipe with the silver peg she pulled out of her voluminous apron. She tamped it down again and studied it. A sliver of a moon peeked out from behind the clouds.

"Well," Aunt Martha said, "she's your child. I reckon you're the only one can protect her. Find her fiancé. He'll help you out. I reckon between the two of you there's enough love for that child to protect her from most anybody."

"Do you think my vision was real?" Annie Laura shook her head. "I don't," she said before Aunt Martha had time to respond. "I think it's naught but a vision brought on by the lightning strike, and I don't set any store in visions."

"Suit yourself, but in my experience, visions are truth laid upon us. What we do with the sight is a measure of our courage."

Annie Laura nodded, her chest hollow.

"There's more?" Aunt Martha probed.

"No, that's all," Annie Laura lied. How could she explain her vision of Leonard when she didn't understand it herself?

"I'll take care of the children," Aunt Martha said. "You get a good night's sleep here, you and that baby I reckon you're carrying, and then come tomorrow, you go find James and take care of your business. Right now, I'm a'going up there to whup Leonard's ass."

"Don't hurt him." It was an automatic response. Annie Laura no longer meant it. She put her hand to her belly.

Aunt Martha peered at her over her corncob pipe. "Do you mean that, or is that something you know you ought to say? Because by now, if he were my husband, he'd be missing a couple of toes."

"The demons that chase Leonard, I don't understand. He was a good man, once. He loved me. I don't know what broke him, but something did, and one day, maybe that something will get fixed."

"Humph," Aunt Martha grunted. "The boy's my own flesh and blood. His mama and I raised him from when he was a baby. He always was stubborn in his ways. You couldn't tell him nothing. But when he was sweet, there weren't no sweeter boy born."

Aunt Martha stood, pulled her pipe from her mouth, wrapped it carefully in a handkerchief, and stowed it in her pocket. "Go on to bed," she said. "The children won't sleep until you do."

Annie Laura lay awake in front of the fire, the sounds of her children's gentle breathing around her. It should have given her a peaceful feeling—there was no better time of the day than when all of her children slept, and she had a few moments of peace, knowing they were all safe and accounted for. But the sweet relief of sleep was denied her.

Leonard. Tears welled in her eyes for the man lost to her, the man she yearned to find. She ached for him in the way of a thirty-eight-year-old woman—part romantic imaginings—mostly overshadowed by her exhaustion and unexpected grief at life turning out different from her dreams.

Leonard—tall, dark-skinned, like some proud warrior. The first time she'd seen him taking a dip in the spring right by his mama's house, his brown skin had glinted in the sunlight through thousands of tiny water droplets pebbling his body like diamonds. He felt her eyes upon him, looked over at her and smiled, his teeth white against that dark skin. He was the tallest man she ever met, and his size made her feel safe. Here was a man who could make all of her dreams come true.

But Leonard grew tired of farming. He didn't love the land as she did. He complained that everything took too long to grow.

He became restless. He fell in with some men somewhere along the way, men much richer than he, and the only way he could forget his poverty—and the fact that his wife was supporting him—was through the drink.

Annie Laura turned a blind eye to it. Maybe it was selfishness on her part, but the long nights of drinking kept him out of her hair so she could raise the children and run the farm in peace instead of running around trying to find something for him to do that would keep him happy. Besides, she believed that deep down inside all of that anger and meanness, he would find his way without her help.

Maybe she could have stopped his foolishness. Maybe she was partially to blame for where he was now. What she did know is that even though she might wish him dead, she still loved him. And that didn't make a bit of sense. She found herself hoping Martha would take care of him. But then she realized that wasn't fair. Why had she sent Martha up to do the business that was hers? She should be the one carrying that shotgun. She should be the one taking off one of his toes to show she meant business.

She sat up from the pallet in front of the warm, cozy fire and searched for her cloak. She stood, tiptoed carefully over the sprawled bodies of her children in peaceful sleep, and silently opened the door gently so as not to wake the children. It creaked when she closed it. She peeked in the window again to see if the children had moved. They had not. Annie Laura ran down the steps and up the hill to her house. She noted she was now running in a straight line. The vertigo was gone.

Aunt Martha would clean up no more of Annie Laura's messes. It was long past time for Annie Laura to deal with Leonard herself.

Clutching her skirts, she ran up the hill. She would know what to do as soon as she got there. The flickering flame of the kerosene lamp in her bedroom window lighted her way through the darkness. Heart beating in her throat, years of anger pressing her forward, she thrust open the front door, and strode into the bedroom.

Aunt Martha stood on one side of the bed aiming her deer rifle at Leonard's chest.

Leonard backed up, his eyes darted to the window. He was about to escape.

Annie Laura knew what she had to do.

She snatched the rifle from Aunt Martha and took careful aim at her husband.

Aunt Martha jumped, held her hand on the barrel of the rifle and hissed, "You got a good wife and a passel of children who are skeered to death of you. Is that the way you want them to grow up? I reckon I ought to just go on ahead and kill you now, put them out of their misery. Annie Laura spends as much money bailing you out of jail as she does on the children and the farm put together. You, nephew, are a liability."

Leonard ignored Martha completely. "Now, Annie Laura, you stop this foolishness now," his words were an attempt to placate her, but his voice shook.

"Not a soul would miss you if I were to shoot you right now. No one would cry at your funeral nor mourn over your grave," Annie Laura said.

"But I promise I'll change. I'm sorry!"

His sickeningly familiar words gave her the courage she needed.

She snatched the barrel away from Aunt Martha's grasp, cocked the gun, aimed, and pulled the trigger.

Leonard hit the floor.

His scream was agony, followed by a moan.

Aunt Martha bent down to examine the damages. She looked up at Annie Laura and grinned. "You always did have good aim."

"Come on, boy. Get up. You ain't dead," Aunt Martha said, "Maybe you'll change your ways."

Leonard moaned.

Annie Laura let out the breath she'd been holding.

"Get ahold of yourself, young'un" Aunt Martha rapped Leonard's head.

"You shot my foot," Leonard whined, jerking away from Aunt Martha. "Why'd you go and shoot my foot? I'm not going to be able to walk nor do any work."

"Well, that ain't unusual. I can't remember the last time you done any work," Aunt Martha said.

"That ain't fair, Aunt Martha, and you know it." Leonard moaned again. "I go out every day of my life and work my fingers to the bones for my young'uns. Why, I fish and hunt and put meat on the table."

"Is that what you tell yourself?" Aunt Martha asked. "And do you believe your own lies?"

"I'm all dizzy from the pain. You're words, they're winding around my head and confusing me," Leonard cried.

"Ok, then," Martha said, "here's a circle for you. It's probably a'going to take a few days for your foot to mend. And don't act like it's more than it is, because it ain't. Worse thing you got is a little scratch and some bruising. If Annie Laura'd a'wanted to shoot your foot off, she would have, but I reckon she just wanted to give you something to think on."

"You blew my toe off," Leonard said. "Look at it. It's bleeding all over the floor."

"You don't need that toe. And don't you be leaving that mess for me nor the young'uns to clean up," Annie Laura said, her voice strong.

"I can't do nothing now. It hurts too bad," Leonard said.

"Oh, I don't reckon you feel it now like you will tomorrow," Aunt Martha said. "Now clean up this here mess while it's not hurting as bad as it will. I'll come check on you tomorrow, and we'll talk more about a plan for you being allowed to stay in this house."

"What do you mean 'a plan for me staying in this house'? This house is mine."

"That's where you're wrong. This house belongs to me and your mama. And the only person who's ever going to get a deed to this house is Annie Laura. And that ain't a'going to happen until I'm dead and gone. So you just think on that."

"Damned old maids," Leonard said.

"You got that right. Neither of us married, didn't want to be forced to hand over our hard-earned land to some sorry husband. So we made do here, raised you, settled the land. And Annie Laura here, well she made it profitable. And you're here where you are because of us, and don't you never forget it. Now I've waited about as long as I'm a'going to wait for you to straighten up and do right by Annie Laura and your children. Do you understand me?"

"I reckon I do."

Of course, what else was he going to say? Annie Laura had to smile at Aunt Martha, a woman not ashamed of her nephew, the baby out of wedlock. Neither she nor her sister gave a damn what others thought. They'd settled the land and birthed Leonard without the encumbrance of a husband, and had done pretty well.

"Here now," Martha said. "Clean up like I said, and then I'll give you a little something to help you sleep."

Leonard groaned. "Annie Laura, you help me clean this. You're my wife, done shot my toe off. The least you can do is help me clean up and tend to me."

"I don't think so. " Annie Laura turned and walked out of the room. When she walked past the window on her way back down to Aunt Martha's, she heard the "swish, swish, swish" of a scrub brush against the wood floor.

She made her way down the hill. She slept a peaceful sleep.

Chapter 7

"Are you sure?" Viola Lee asked, working hard to keep the panic from her voice.

Mr. Tiller, the kindly postmaster, rifled through the sheaf of mail on his counter. "I'm sorry, Viola Lee," he said, worry creasing his forehead, "nothing today."

She needed to hear from James. He could take her away and help her sort through all of this confusion. They would create their own happy home and their children would never, ever suffer the fear of living without knowing all they needed to know about their very own parents. Their children would be safe and secure knowing that their real mama and daddy lived right there with them. Forever.

" How long has it been since you've heard from him?"

"Nearly three weeks," Viola Lee rubbed her burning nose. She turned away before the tears fell. "I'm sure he's fine." She clasped her reticule in one hand and her parasol in the other. "Thank you." Where was James? Maybe, he was just around the corner, ready to surprise her.

"I'll keep looking," Mr. Tiller called after her. "I'll send someone out if anything comes. Don't worry," he said.

But he didn't sound at all confident in his words, and Viola Lee was quite certain that James was not fine. She needed a letter from him to explain why he hadn't arrived on Saturday as they had planned. What if he had been injured in a logging accident? Or worse. What if he discovered that they were kin? She pushed the thought out of her head. She had to think rationally.

Two months ago, James left to take a job with a logging company. For the first month, James never went more than two days without writing. He yearned to learn proper grammar, and every letter he sent, Viola Lee would correct his grammar, writing explanations so that he would understand what he was doing wrong. She would send the letter back along with a letter of her own filled with the news from Grassy Glade and the inconsequential happenings in her own life.

She needed him to reassure her that all he wanted was her. She needed reassurance that he was looking forward to their life together just as much as she was. If she closed her eyes, she could hear him speak.

And then that ugly thought intruded.

But it wasn't true. It couldn't be.

Was her dream of a happy life together going to be just that? A dream?

Maybe she was just scared because of his logging job. It was dangerous work, and she'd not had a good feeling about it from the outset. She'd heard too many horror stories.

"I don't want you going," Viola Lee had said.

"But I need to," James responded, taking her small hand in his large, capable one. His hand was so different from the hands of the boys at school. Their hands were soft and white. James's hands were dark, strong, the calluses thick from farming, from cutting wood, from making his way. His life had been hard. Orphaned at two, raised by a kind aunt with too many mouths to feed, James had been forced to earn his own way when he was nine years old. James was tough. He would come home to her. No matter what.

Unless he was dead.

And who would be alerted if it were so? Who was his next of kin? Who was it that James might have put down on his papers if there were such papers?

She had to stop thinking this way. These thoughts would only lead to heartache. She had a much more immediate concern. If James showed up today and they married on Saturday, would it be incest?

The horrible word tasted like bile in her mouth.

She needed to do some research. She needed to first find out who her own father was. And then, ask him if he had any other children.

That seemed simple enough.

But who was her father? And who would tell her about her father?

She had an idea.

She walked quickly back home and tiptoed up the front steps. She stood on the porch, silent, listening. She could hear Mary Scarlett helping a customer pick out the right material for her daughter's dress.

"I think this pink calico is perfect," she heard her mother say, "and it just came in today."

"Esther does look good in pink," the woman said. "Do you have any lace that matches?"

The voices disappeared into the back of the store.

Perfect, Viola Lee thought. She snuck into her mother's bedroom, opened the creaky cedar chest that sat at the foot of her bed, and dug down deep for her grandmother's Bible. She only knew it was there because her mother had mentioned it; Viola Lee herself never had any interest in old things. Until today. Maybe, just maybe, the Bible would record the name of Viola Lee's father.

She pushed through baby clothes, an old Confederate soldier uniform, and Mary Scarlett's own wedding gown before she reached the bottom of the chest. She felt around, touching the bottom of the chest front to back and side to side.

No Bible.

Where could it be?

Viola Lee put everything back into the chest, closed the top, and pulled open the top bureau drawer. She rifled through her mother's papers, jewelry, and undergarments, but did not find the Bible. She closed the drawer and looked around the room for the next possible hiding place.

Suddenly, she heard footsteps. The door between the kitchen and the store creaked open, and Mary Scarlett entered the kitchen.

"Viola Lee?" she called.

Viola Lee froze.

Her mother walked across to Viola Lee's bedroom and called again.

Viola Lee crawled under Mary Scarlett's bed.

Mary Scarlett's footsteps sounded down the hallway. She stepped into her bedroom and called once again. "Viola Lee?"

She went to the window, raised the sash, and called out into the back garden. "John Sebring, have you seen Viola Lee?"

"No," John called. "Last I knew she was headed to the post office to check on a letter from James."

"Well, if you see her, will you tell her I'm looking for her? I need her to try on her wedding dress."

"I'll tell her," John called.

Mary Scarlett closed the sash, sighed, and sat on the bed. The springs creaked and brushed Viola Lee's nose. Viola Lee's quick intake of breath was silenced by more creaking springs as Mary Scarlett removed first one shoe and then the other and rubbed her feet. It had never occurred to Viola Lee that Mary Scarlett's feet may ache after standing on them all day in the store. She felt a stab of compassion for her adopted mother, who never complained about her work in the store, though she had no problem complaining about everything else.

It was the money she earned at the store that kept them afloat. Viola Lee knew this, though she didn't think of it often. John Sebring kept them in fish and fresh vegetables, but it was the income from Mary Scarlett's store that enabled them to live in this house and bought Viola Lee new clothes.

Viola Lee was just beginning to feel something other than anger at Mary Scarlett when her eye caught on something just above her.

Jammed between the mattress and the bedsprings in the dead center of the bed lay the family Bible, hidden from everyone except Viola Lee.

It seemed to take forever for Mary Scarlett to stop rubbing her feet, put her shoes on, and head back to her work at the store. The minute Viola Lee heard the kitchen door close, she slid from beneath the bed, wiped away the dust bunnies gathered in the folds of her skirt, and rolled back the mattress.

She held the black leather-bound Bible in her hands.

And now, where to read it?

She wrapped it in her apron and bolted out the side door, calling to John Sebring, "I'm going to the church to practice." It was the perfect decoy. She played the organ for church, though neither of her parents attended, and spent a few hours every week practicing the old pump organ.

She ran down the road before he could answer her and beckon to her to come talk to Mary Scarlett.

And, it wasn't really a lie. She often sought solace in her music, the one thing she could count on to make her feel better. She could pour her heart out over the keys; the words to the old hymns never failed to soothe her.

She hoped the church would be open and she could be alone. She walked down the dusty road that led from her house, past the post office to the church. The early morning sun danced in the oak leaves and dappled the gray sand. She skirted past Mr. Anderson, who was sweeping the wood sidewalk in front of his general store, and then walked down the empty road between his store and the church.

The gray clapboard church stood in need of a coat of paint, the cemetery behind it shaded with mossy oak trees, and the sparkling blue North Bay spread out beyond. Viola Lee walked carefully up the steep wooden stairs, slick with green moss that they couldn't seem to get rid of no matter how often they scrubbed it. She opened the oak door and headed for the organ, her steps making the wood floors creak. Had someone climbed the stairs after her, perhaps one of the church ladies there for the Monday morning tidy-up? But when she looked back, there was no one. She was alone.

And then a thought occurred to her. What if James came? Right here, right now? What if he came and sat down beside her, and they could figure this mystery out together. Wouldn't that be wonderful?

She slipped into the front pew. It creaked as she sat down. She unwrapped her apron and opened the Bible. Her hands shook and she felt her heart beat in her ears, as if she were holding a giant conch shell to listen to the ocean, only this wasn't the ocean. This was fear.

She turned the thin pages, Genesis, Exodus, Leviticus. She stopped. She knew the family registry was in the Psalms but she couldn't make her hands go there. She took a deep breath. She swallowed.

She opened the Bible to the family registry, ran her finger down three pages of births, marriages, and deaths. Until she came to her own birth.

Viola Lee Blakely: Mother: unknown German woman. Father: Walter Blakely.

And in squiggly, handwritten parenthesis: Adopted: 14 January 1899 by Mary Scarlett and John Sebring Morgan.

Her face felt hot, and her legs too weak to stand on. So she was the daughter of the odious man on the ferry. Walter Blakely. She had imagined something completely other, a first love, perhaps the marriage forbidden by the family; or, she had imagined, perhaps her mother and father had been tragically separated and still secretly loved one another and would one day find each other again.

But not this. Her birth mother hated this man, her father. She could see it on her face and hear it in her voice in their encounter on the ferry.

What had he said? *Are you still whoring?*

Was it true? Had her mother been a prostitute? Was she a child conceived and born in sin? Had John Sebring and Mary Scarlett saved her from a life of shame?

Now, more than ever, she needed the solace of her music.

She shuffled through *The Evangel* hymnal and turned to her favorite, page 132, "He Will Not Forsake You."

She heard the floor creak once again. Her heart fluttered. Please let it be James. But when she looked up, no one was there. The wood floor did that sometimes, settling of its own accord. Pastor said it was because the ground below it was soft, close enough to the bay for the sand to shift with the tides sometimes. Viola Lee didn't believe him. She thought a sinkhole was more likely. Viola Lee had seen a sinkhole swallow someone's garden when she was younger.

She settled herself at the organ, lost herself in the lilting rhythm, pumping the organ with her feet, her hands dancing across the keys. *He who feeds the raven, and numbers every star, will not let his children one hour forgotten be.*

She prayed her thanks, that her loving God would not forget her James, that as his eye was on the raven, his eye would surely be on James, protecting, loving him.

She played the hymn again, the door creaked open, but she didn't stop to look. She knew it would be either Mrs. Jackson or Mrs. Anderson, tidying up, checking that the hymnbooks were neatly arranged on the holders in the backs of the wood pews, and the fans, compliments of Wilson Funeral Home, were neatly arranged in a wood box at the rear of the sanctuary. Though it was yet early spring, the days could turn hot all of a sudden, and the ladies were always prepared. She told herself this to keep from getting overly excited at the prospect that it might be James come home.

Viola Lee lost herself in the promise of the chorus: *Trust him, trust him, whose glories shine afar; He will not forsake you Who numbers every star.*

She smiled and allowed the precious peace to ease her mind, relax her spirit. The Lord would watch after her James. She closed her eyes and let her fingers find the familiar keys.

"You really believe all that rubbish?" a male voice shocked her from her rhapsody. Her fingers slipped from the keys, and her eyes sprang open.

It was not James.

Chapter 8

The man, wearing a rumpled linen suit and an expensive, though grease-stained hat, sat on the front pew just a few feet from the organ. His hat remained on his head though they sat in the house of God.

He smiled with his mouth but not his eyes when she stared at the offensive hat.

"Play," he said. "I like to hear you play. The words are rubbish, but the music is passable."

She stared at him. A cold chill ran through her. He looked familiar. She wished the Monday morning ladies would come soon. He was scary.

"No," she said. "I've finished with my practicing. If it's the preacher you wish to speak to, I'll be happy to go get him." There was something familiar about the man. She put her hands back on the organ keys.

"I thought you said you were finished practicing," he said, mocking her.

And suddenly, she realized who the man was.

Walter Blakely. She felt like she needed to throw up. Instead, she creased the pages of the hymnal, adjusting it so it would stay open.

In the silence that followed she could hear him breathing, heavy, rasping. Her hands shook. She wished her daddy was here. She tried to think. What had she been playing? She turned the pages of the hymnal searching for something familiar. What did Walter Blakely want from her?

She turned to see him seated on the front pew, uncomfortably close to the organ bench, his face a mottled, angry red. She tried to make her voice sound firm, but she had that feeling like she was in a dream and the land beneath her a mirage.

"I think you need to leave," she said.

Her heart pounded, and she could taste danger like a film of smoke lying heavy in the room.

Suddenly, Walter Blakely sprang forward. Viola Lee shrank back, her hand landing on the organ keys, the sound dying like a muffled cat. She was trapped. His thick hands squeezed her shoulders. He breathed in great rasping breaths.

Then, like an afterthought, he laughed, and released his grip.

It was all the time she needed. Viola Lee ducked down and away from Walter Blakely, slid across the organ bench, and scrabbled to the wooden floor. Her legs felt weak, but she forced them to move. Snatching up her skirts, she hurtled down the aisle, pushed open the door, and was nearly blinded by the bright morning sun.

She closed her eyes, opened them, ran down the steps, slipped on the moss of the third step, fell on her knees, tripped by her bunched-up skirt. She yanked the skirt high above her knees, heedless of anyone seeing every inch of her legs and undergarments. She lowered her head and ran faster than she had ever run before. She skidded to a stop, but not before knocking the basket out of Ruth Merritt's hand—calico, thread, needles, and pins flying across the dusty road.

"Viola Lee!" Ruth, her best friend, said. She clutched Viola Lee's shaking shoulders and looked her full in the face. "You look like you've seen a ghost!" Ruth looked back to see what was pursuing Viola Lee. "What are you running from?"

"I'm so..."—Viola Lee tried to catch her breath—"...sorry." She breathed heavily and looked back, but there was no one pursuing her. "A man," Viola Lee said.

Ruth's eyes widened. "What man? Who?" Ruth flipped open her fan and waved it across Viola Lee's face in huge, fluttering arcs.

"I don't know who he was," Viola Lee said and leaned down, gathering the packet of pins, threaded needle, and piece of bright red calico, now gray with dust. Viola Lee shook out the material and rubbed it against her own dress. "There," she said, "I think I knocked off most of the dust." She could not for the life of her tell even her best friend Ruth that the man in the church was Walter Blakely, her birth father. Shame turned her cheeks scarlet.

Ruth reached for the white fabric that had landed miraculously unsullied on a hitching post. She smiled and pulled it down. "No harm done," she said. Then she looked up at Viola Lee.

Viola Lee checked over her shoulder again, but Blakely was not after her. She knew she had not imagined the encounter. She'd been warned of drifters in the area, ne'er-do-wells who wandered from place to place, but she'd never encountered one, never considered the church as a place where one might wander in. Only this wasn't some anonymous drifter. She was still shaking.

Ruth took her hand. "Come on," she said. "Mama will make you some peppermint tea."

It was Mrs. Merritt's answer to everything that ailed you, and more often than not, it worked.

Viola Lee's world had just collapsed in upon itself. First her fear for James, and then the horrifying discovery that her birth father was this frightening man. She placed a hand on her shoulder where he had grasped her, tried to wipe away the memory. But it was there. It wouldn't go away.

The moment she sat down in Mrs. Merritt's sunny white kitchen with its gay blue and white curtains flapping in the morning breeze, and sniffed the scent of freshly baked bread and peppermint tea, a bubble rose in her throat. She tried to swallow it, fearing she would vomit on Mrs. Merritt's crisp white tablecloth with jolly cross-stitched forks, knives, and spoons, worked in blue. She grasped the tablecloth to steady herself, rumpling its newly starched perfection. She squeezed her eyes shut, tried blinking away the memory.

But it would not go away.

The moment she told Mrs. Merritt what happened, Mrs. Merritt jumped up from the table and called out to her husband. "Joe?"

She wiped her hands on her apron and strode out the back door, her bulk making her steps heavy. "*Joe!*" she hollered to her husband, who was out back tending to the cows.

Mr. Merritt appeared at the door, splashed his face with the cool water he poured from the pitcher into the washbowl, and wiped it with the clean towel hanging beside it.

"Happy to have an excuse to come in," he said, smiling, but when he looked up at the three women in the room, his face fell. "What is it?" he asked.

"Joe," Mrs. Merritt said, "there is a ne'er-do-well, a tramp, come to town, and he accosted our Viola Lee."

"What?" he asked, shaking his head as if he hadn't heard right.

Viola Lee cleared the bubble from her throat, wanted to assure him she was fine, but more than anything, and she didn't understand why, she wanted to assure him that she was unsullied. "He didn't choke me or anything," she said.

"*Choked* you?" Mr. Merritt asked, aghast. "I'm going after the sheriff, right now."

"I'm not hurt," Viola Lee said. "He *didn't* choke me. He only squeezed my shoulder. He frightened me. Surprised me, more like." What if they found out that the man who had done this was actually her birth father? Then what would happen? Would she somehow be to blame? She didn't know the laws regarding blood fathers and their children.

But what if he came after her again, and this time, she couldn't run? This time, she couldn't get away?

"I need to use the outhouse...," she said and rushed outside, reaching to open the half-moon door. Before she could shove the door out of her way, she vomited onto the ground.

Mrs. Merritt came running with a cool wet washcloth. She wiped Viola Lee's face tenderly.

"I'm sorry," Viola Lee said.

"Oh, sweetie, you have nothing to be sorry for. My Joe and the sheriff will find this man, wherever he has gone, and will bring him to justice."

Viola Lee wanted to say thank you, and be polite, but the emotions inside threatened to tumble out again, and as she wasn't sure what form they would take, she held her peace.

"No," she said. "Don't send after the sheriff. I'm sure the man is long gone now."

Mrs. Merritt studied Viola Lee's face. Viola Lee felt she could see right through her, could read her mind.

"Help her home, Ruth," Mrs. Merritt said. "She needs to tell her parents and then lie down. But wait just a moment before you go."

Mrs. Merritt hurried inside. Viola Lee heard the sound of a drawer opening, and then Mrs. Merritt came down the back porch steps and handed Viola Lee a lavender sachet. "You put that right beside you when you sleep. It will help you have sweet dreams."

Viola Lee nodded her thanks, trying to smile.

"Go on, now," Mrs. Merritt said. But there was a questioning look on her face.

But when they got to her house, Viola Lee stopped Ruth from walking up the front steps.

She remembered the hushed conversation between her parents.

She remembered that Mary Scarlett wanted to protect her brother.

"I can't trust her."

Chapter 9

Viola Lee and Ruth stood frozen at the bottom of the porch steps leading up to Viola Lee's house.

Viola Lee was embarrassed by the tears that rose again in her eyes and spilled down her face. She was embarrassed that her life was such a wreck. Why couldn't she have a normal life like Ruth? Two perfect parents, a perfect house. Ruth's mother worked inside the home, and Ruth's father was a dairy farmer. He provided the milk for nearly the entire town of Grassy Glade, or at least for those who didn't have their own cows. Ruth's brother made the horse and wagon milk deliveries. That was normal.

Her life was not. Not only had her birth father just scared the sense out of her, he was a criminal. Furthermore, it was Mary Scarlett who ran a store and brought in the family's income, not John Sebring. That was not normal.

She bet Annie Laura would never run a store. She was a good wife, took care of her children, and stayed in the house cooking, managing things. Maybe she had a henhouse and a little kitchen garden. Her husband was a farmer, like Mr. Merritt, a man whom she loved deeply and who loved Annie Laura. She bet Annie Laura's husband provided for the family so that her real mother could do the job that God gave her: raising her children with love and kindness.

Unless she was *a whore*. Viola Lee squelched the thought like a fat mosquito, slapped it right down and squished it. Annie Laura might be a lot of things, but she wasn't a whore. Viola Lee knew that in the center of her being.

When she was a mother, her children would never know what worries and cares she had known when she was just a child—she had been responsible for keeping house. What kind of mother lets a child keep house at age seven?

It was true, she had enjoyed it, had enjoyed being considered all grown up when she was just seven. Why hadn't her daddy stopped it?

That was enough. She had to get over this pity party. She needed to breathe some fresh air and figure out what to do next.

She raised her chin and took Ruth's arm, and strode away from her home.

"Where are we going?" Ruth asked.

"Away from here," Viola Lee said, her chin jutting forward.

Ruth took her hand.

The sun was warm on their faces, and Viola Lee led the way away from her house, down the dirt road that led to the bay. The girls had picnicked there often enough, but this would be the first time they'd gone without plans.

Viola Lee wanted to sit by the bay. It helped her to think. But she wanted to be where people could hear her if she needed help. She chose a place near the ferry landing. A pier stretched out beside the landing, and the pier pilings were a good place to hide in plain sight.

Ruth followed her and they settled down on the white sand beneath the first massive creosote-smelling pine piling.

They sat quiet long enough for tiny fiddler crabs to emerge from their hiding places. They moved in jerky movements, like the matchstick and thread spool toys her father made with rubber bands. Ruth and Viola Lee sat still, watching them scurry awkwardly about.

Ruth sneezed, and the fiddler crabs disappeared into small holes, holes that seemed way too small for their bodies.

"I wonder what they eat?" Viola Lee asked, breaking the silence.

"See those little sand pellets?" Ruth asked her.

The sand pellets were hard to miss as they surrounded each fiddler crab's hole.

"They eat the sand," Ruth said, "and then spit it back out again."

"Why would they do that?" Viola Lee asked.

"I don't know," she said. "Must be something good-tasting inside that sand. Maybe they extract the good and then spit out the bad. Whatever it is, they keep coming back and doing it over and over again."

"Kind of like my daddy," Viola Lee said. "I don't know why he stays married to my mama, except that he doesn't believe in divorce, and he says he loves her. I reckon he takes in her sand, extracts the tiny good particle, then spits out the rest."

Ruth laughed at Viola Lee. "You say the funniest things," she said, but her laughter was good-natured, and Viola Lee felt she meant it as a compliment.

"I reckon the best thing I could do right now is to find my daddy. I'll tell him about the man and see what he thinks ought to be done."

Ruth looked at her. "You're mighty brave, Viola Lee," Ruth said. "I know after what's happened to you today, I wouldn't be able to think straight. Where do you think your daddy is?"

"Well," she said, "he's usually either fishing, tending to the garden, or carrying people to the ferry in his car. He didn't go fishing today because I saw his pole sitting up on the porch before I left this morning. He was in the garden earlier swearing outside my window."

Ruth laughed. John Sebring's swearing was a burden to all the womenfolk of the town, except Mary Scarlett—and Ruth and Viola Lee, who loved learning new swear words from him. Not that they would ever say them aloud. It was just nice to have a store of them in their heads to use when they got really angry and couldn't say anything out loud. Cursing silently helped make them feel a whole lot better.

"I did notice that when we walked up the porch," Viola Lee continued, "his car was gone."

"So if we wait here long enough, we're bound to see him?" Ruth asked.

Viola Lee nodded. "Yep, and there he is now."

She jumped up, with Ruth following her, and ran to greet her father.

"Hey, girl!" John Sebring Morgan lifted Viola Lee in his strong arms and swirled her around like she was a little girl. He coaxed a laugh out of her.

"Daddy!" Viola Lee said. No matter how bad things were, he could make her laugh, forget the bad stuff. It was his gift, and he practiced it without even realizing it. Viola Lee suspected it was the reason he could live so happily with Mary Scarlett.

"What brings you girls down here?" he asked. "Watching the waves roll in to pass the time?"

Viola Lee chewed the inside of her bottom lip. Ruth looked at her, expectant. Ruth wanted her to tell her daddy about the choking. Viola Lee cleared her throat and swallowed.

"I got something I need to tell you," she said.

"Well," he said, "go on, then. But let me buy you an ice cream cone while you tell me. They have some today down at the train depot. I saw it when I dropped off my last customers."

Ice cream allowed Viola Lee to feel like the little child she was never allowed to be with Mary Scarlett. Mary Scarlett treated her like an adult from the time she could understand simple commands. Sweep the floor. Wash the dishes. Empty the stove.

Ruth nodded to Viola Lee. "Go ahead," she whispered as John Sebring turned around and strode toward his car to take them to get some ice cream. "Tell him."

"I will," Viola Lee hissed back, "but maybe not now."

Ruth shook her head. Telling John Sebring bad news was never easy. He did not like to hear the bad stuff.

"He needs to know," Ruth said.

"What is it you girls are whispering about back there?" John Sebring asked, turning around and smiling. His blue eyes shone brightly in his pleasant, red-cheeked face. Some of Viola Lee's friends thought he was the real Santa Claus when she was little, because he was always distributing nickels for ice cream to children passing by his front porch running errands for their mamas.

"Nothing, Daddy," Viola Lee said and caught his hand, swinging it as they walked to the car. Ruth caught up with them, scowling at Viola Lee.

They climbed into the car and, with a jerk and a jolt, the car lurched forward. The bumpy ride made talking difficult, for which Viola Lee was grateful.

They reached the train depot and the car chugged to a stop, gave a cough, and John Sebring let the engine die.

"There's something Viola Lee needs to tell you," Ruth said. Her voice came out shaky, and Viola Lee pinched her arm, but Ruth ignored her.

"What is it?" John Sebring studied Viola Lee's face. "What is it you want to tell me?"

Viola Lee was mute. She didn't know how to put the words together to say what needed saying.

"I got folks to pick up," he said, his tone friendly. He pulled out his gold pocket watch, opened it, checked the time, and closed it back, stowing it deep in his front pocket. "But we still have an hour. What's on your mind?"

Ruth nudged her again.

Finally, Ruth burst out. "A man grabbed her in the church this morning."

John Sebring leapt from the front seat, opened the back door, and pulled Viola Lee out of the car. "Child," he said, "what is she talking about?"

Tears of frustration, anger at Ruth, and fear of what her father might reveal about Walter Blakely choked Viola Lee. She couldn't speak, and John Sebring gently brushed the hair from her neck. "Come on, sweet girl, stand out here in the sun so I can see."

She obliged, and when he saw the angry red fingermarks on her shoulder, he bellowed, "Who did this to you?"

People at the depot looked up and studied John Sebring and Viola Lee.

"Daddy," she said, "I don't want everybody looking at me." She hated the tears that streamed down her face, hated that she was so weak that she let herself be strangled. Why had she chosen to go to the church? If she hadn't been there, it would never have happened. And then a chilling thought came to her. What if Walter Blakely had been following her?

"I think she's afraid to go home," Ruth filled in, seeing that Viola Lee was not going to speak for herself.

A look that Viola Lee had never seen crossed her father's face. It was a series of emotions. His eyes opened wide with surprise. Then he closed his eyes, breathed deeply, his lips tightening, his jaw jutting forward. His eyes narrowed with cold clarity. A muscle in his face twitched. But just as quickly, his face cleared and he wore his normal pleasant smile. "That's not possible," he said, brushing off Ruth's words like he would have brushed a mosquito off his arm.

But the series of emotions on her father's face had told her more than she wanted to know. Her father knew something and was hiding it. Because he didn't want to confront it, didn't want to admit it, he pretended it didn't exist. It was how her father got through life. Mary Scarlett dealt with real-life matters like paying the bills and planning for the future.

Viola Lee no longer wanted ice cream. "You don't believe me?" she said.

Her father swung around and looked at her. "Yes, child. I believe you."

Viola Lee trembled, and this time it was anger, not fear. "Are you going to do anything about it?" she asked.

"I'll do what I can," he said.

Ruth's eyes widened.

"Come on, Ruth," she said. "Let's go home." Though she didn't really want to go to her home.

"Don't you worry," Ruth said to Viola Lee once they were out of John Sebring's earshot. "My daddy is going to find the sheriff. They'll take care of that tramp."

That's exactly what Viola Lee feared.

She needed James. Nothing could give her more pleasure than to have him appear at the end of the road in his red lumberman's shirt to swoop in and protect her. But he wasn't here. Ruth was.

Ruth was silent for most of the walk, but once they reached the front yard path, she pulled at Viola Lee's hand. "We are going to pray, right now," she said.

Viola Lee nodded. They gripped hands, and Ruth prayed.

"Dear Lord, you are our friend, and our protector, and we do not know what is behind that door, but you do. I pray that you would prepare us and strengthen us. Give us a spirit of fearlessness. And protect our Viola Lee. In your holy name we pray, Amen."

Viola Lee felt her throat tighten. She swallowed, took Ruth's hand, and they set out. They walked to the front door once again, Viola Lee, with a fearlessness that she did not feel. But she knew that she had to pretend and maybe, like sometimes happened, if she believed it for long enough, it would become true. Or maybe God would step in and help her out.

The house was silent. She walked through the front door. Looked around as if she were in a stranger's home. The room looked as it always did. Fresh flowers she'd picked yesterday were on the table. The azaleas were drooping, their papery thin pink bells falling in upon themselves.

The grandfather clock ticked its slow reminder of *tempus fugit*, the fancy letters on the face of the clock reminding everyone who walked by to take care, to be wise, to appreciate and remember each moment because soon it will be gone. Viola Lee could only hope this moment would be soon gone.

The green silk-covered settee sat empty, the lacy crocheted antimacassar resting undisturbed across its back.

Beside the front door, a man's greasy hat settled on the hat rack, a hat that did not belong to her father or anyone else she knew.

Where was the stranger? Mary Scarlett's rules were firm. They entertained guests in this, the front room. No one but family was allowed in the back of the house, and surely this man wasn't family.

A locked door led from Mary Scarlett's dry goods store to their kitchen, making it easy for her to transition back and forth from her sewing and crocheting at the kitchen table to tending the customers that came to her store. The door outside the store had said "Closed." Mary Scarlett always opened the door on time. What was different about today? Who was this visitor who wielded such power as to shut the store down?

"Listen," Ruth said.

Viola Lee heard voices out back near the kitchen garden and well. A man's voice and the murmuring response of Mary Scarlett. Ruth slipped her hand in Viola Lee's again, and they walked through the kitchen and out the back door.

Mary Scarlett, her tall, strong adopted mother, held her hands out in supplication, pleading like a child. That scared Viola Lee more than being choked. Nothing and nobody cowed Mary Scarlett. What had happened?

The man's face was set in an unyielding smile.

"Please, Walter," Mary Scarlett said. "You can't."

"Yes," he said, "I can." He looked up and saw Viola Lee and Ruth. "Why, look! There's the little piece now."

Mary Scarlett looked up to see Viola Lee and Ruth. "Go on, now," she said to Viola Lee. "This is none of your concern. Git."

"You ain't easy scared, are you?" he asked, cocking his head. "Thought I might of scared some life into you this morning." And he leaned his head back and roared with his own laughter again.

"You don't have any business here or with her," Mary Scarlett said. "Now, leave us alone."

"You really think that, do you, sister?" he said. "After our little contract, what would give you the right to say anything? Don't be going all high and mighty on me, now."

Sweat dripped down Viola Lee's back and she trembled. A memory flashed before her. Her daddy shouting at someone to leave, and Mary Scarlett taking her into her room and locking the door. A man beating on her window, his face emblazoned in her memory, returning only in her nightmares. Until now.

A gunshot startled them all.

Viola Lee turned to see John Sebring standing on the back porch, a shotgun in his hand, aimed at Walter.

"You are trespassing, Blakely," he said. "I'll give you to the count of five to get off my property."

Blakely looked up at him and smiled. "You mean Mary Scarlett's property?"

"Five," John Sebring said. "Four," he said and cocked the shot gun. "Three," he said and took aim. "Two," he said.

Viola Lee's heart pounded. She had never seen her daddy look mean, but right now, he was set to kill.

"Back away, girls," he said.

Viola Lee, Mary Scarlett, and Ruth scattered, and Walter Blakely ran.

John Sebring fired into the ground where Blakely had stood.

Walter Blakely must have felt the spray of dirt. "Shit!" he said, running towards the road. "You trying to kill me?"

"Yes," John Sebring said and cocked the gun.

Viola Lee, Mary, and Ruth huddled together on the side of the house. Viola Lee held her breath so she could hear the running footsteps of Walter Blakely, the clank of the front gate, the squeak of leather, the "clop-clop, clippity-clop" of a horse fading into the distance, and then silence.

They waited for John Sebring to come and tell them all was safe. When he did not, Mary Scarlett led them cautiously around the back of the house. The back porch was empty and John's gun leaned against the doorpost.

They walked slowly, cautiously, into the living room.

John Sebring sat in his favorite chair, a glass of ice water beside him, reading the paper.

Chapter 10

"What's the matter with Daddy?" Jessie asked. He held three-year-old John Wesley in his arms. The children, dressed and fed, stood on Aunt Martha's front porch, door wide open, waiting for Annie Laura and Louise to wash the last of their breakfast dishes so they could go home.

Annie Laura dried the final dish and peered out the open window. In the gray dawn of early morning, Aunt Martha helped Leonard hobble up the cabin stairs. Annie Laura wasn't ready for this. She had nothing to say to Leonard. The night's rest had given her a new energy. Things could never be the same between them. She would leave today to find James. The ride would give her plenty of thinking time. Aunt Martha would understand, though maybe not her urgency. She'd told her she would plant the fields first and then go. But the land didn't have the pull on her today that it usually did. The land felt heavy on her, and she needed to get away from it, too.

"He done gone and hurt his foot," Aunt Martha said to Jessie, maneuvering Leonard up the rickety stairs and onto the porch. Leonard stared straight ahead, like he was walking in his sleep, and Annie Laura wondered what sort of herbs Aunt Martha had concocted for him. "I'm a'having to doctor him down here at my house. Would you mind holding that rocking chair for your daddy?"

The children watched wide-eyed as their dazed daddy limped across the porch, guided by the strong arm of Aunt Martha. Jessie held the chair still, shrinking back away as his daddy eased himself down and into the chair. Aunt Martha left him there by himself on the porch and ushered the children inside, closing the door behind her.

"Is he going to stay here with you?" Louise asked.

"Yes ma'am, I reckon he is. Your mama has got her hands full taking care of all you young'uns. Now, you help her out all you can, you hear me? She's got a week of planting ahead of her, and she needs all the help you can give her."

Annie Laura knew it was time to speak up.

"I'm going to take a little trip, children," she said.

"Where, Mama?" Jessie asked. "Can I go with you?"

"No, son," Annie Laura said, clasping him to her side. "I got to do this on my own. It might take a couple of days. Louise, do you think you can handle things for two whole days and nights?"

Louise's eyes were big. Annie Laura shot a glance at Aunt Martha, who took but a moment to recover from her surprise at this sudden decision.

"Louise, you're going to be in charge while your mama's gone, do you hear me? If you need something, you come right on down here and get it. Your grandma should be back from her doctoring by then."

Annie Laura could have cried with relief. What would she have done all these years without Aunt Martha and Grandma Mary?

"Yes, ma'am," Louise said, her voice tremulous. The sight of her weakened daddy frightened her. "Could you ask Grandma to come up and see us when she gets home?"

"As soon as she rests a little," Aunt Martha said.

Leonard groaned from the front porch, and Annie Laura distanced herself from the door. She didn't want to face him right now. There would be plenty of time for talk later.

"You go on out that back door," Aunt Martha said. "You got plenty to do getting ready for this trip. I'll take care of him. He'll be fit as a fiddle in a couple of days."

"Thank you."

"Don't mention it," she said. "Raising a nephew takes longer than you think." Her eyes danced with a mischievous smile.

Annie Laura laughed and shook her head. "You won't do."

Aunt Martha laughed. Annie Laura kissed her cheek and made her way out. She stopped with her hand on the door and looked back at Aunt Martha. Sudden tears choked her voice. "I do love him," she said, surprised by her own words.

"I know you do, child. It's your gift and your burden. Go on, now. I'll take care of him. I won't hurt him."

Annie Laura nodded, held the door open for her children as they filed out in a solemn line. She closed the door softly behind them and led her children home.

The sun rose pink over the hill, dew glistened on the ground, and her house rose before her like a reward. She stopped and admired the new whitewash, the oak trees standing like sentries on either side, the rose bushes growing up the trellises and around the back porch. Her kitchen garden lay in neat rows with healing herbs already turning green in the early spring light. Soon there would be flowers for the kitchen table, summer squash, melons, and sweet-smelling lavender to sew into little bags and line her drawers. She was blessed.

She hugged John Wesley and picked him up. She pointed to a red-cockaded woodpecker pecking a morning tattoo on the old cypress tree. "He's letting us know we're going to have plenty of firewood for the winter," Annie Laura said.

"How come?" Jessie asked.

"Because when the woodpecker pecks the tree, it means the tree branch is dead or dying," Louise said. "He don't peck unless there are insects gone come out, and insects don't much come out of living trees."

"Is that true, Mama?" Jessie asked.

"That's true," Annie Laura answered.

Jessie peered up at the tall gray cypress. "But I don't want it to die. It's been here my whole life, and the field won't look the same without it."

The other children giggled, but Annie Laura shushed them with a look. "It's always sad when a tree dies, son. But it's good to be warm when the wind starts blowing in the winter, don't you think?"

"Yes, ma'am, I reckon," Jessie said and kicked the dirt in front of him.

"Stop that," Louise said. "You're getting dirt all over me."

"Come on, children. Let's go inside and get ready. It'll be time for school before you know it."

Louise groaned, but Jessie smiled. Jessie liked school. The only one who stayed home was the youngest, John Wesley.

And soon, the baby growing inside of her would be a playmate for John Wesley. She prayed that the lightning strike did no harm.

~

Aunt Martha insisted that Annie Laura use her horse to find James. The mare was slow but sure-footed. Annie Laura rubbed the side of her neck, and they meandered down the clay road headed north. The cold front brought in by yesterday's storm meant a pleasantly cool ride, though warmer by afternoon. She fastened her wool hat more securely on her head and knotted her crocheted shawl, a gift from her dear friend, Margaret, the year before she died in the great fire. The fire had taken Margaret's infant daughter as well and had left John Sebring Morgan a young widower. His grief and his friendship were merged into one in Annie's mind.

The memories of that horrible year ached. It was the year she had unknowingly given up all rights to her daughter.

But that was the past, and nothing could be done about it. This was the present, and there was something she could do. If Walter Blakely was telling the truth, he was James' father. James could not marry Viola Lee. Annie Laura prayed it was not so. But it was up to her to find out the truth.

The horse plodded on, stopping occasionally to get a drink from a roadside drinking trough in one tiny settlement after another. The land grants in West Florida had been generous to prosperous investors, and people came in droves, lured by newspaper articles that mentioned the water and flowers, but not the biting bugs, the varmints, the inferno-like summers, and the bone-aching winters. Only the strong and desperate could survive.

The Waterfall postmaster had given Annie Laura the name of the local Woodmen of America representative, John C. Clark. She found Mr. Clark in a makeshift camp beside a clear, spring-fed creek. He sent her north about five miles to the last timber camp in Florida, deep in the swamps, almost to Alabama. The timber had been left there earlier because conditions were too harsh for the company foremen, Clark reported.

"Bad things going on in there, miss," he said. "I wouldn't go in there alone if I were you."

"I got business to attend to," Annie Laura said. "Thank you for your help."

He shook his head and gave her a rough map of where he thought the camp must be. "This was given to me by the only man who has made it out yet and I've been able to help."

"Help from what?" she asked.

"Help to escape the timber bosses," he said.

"Why can't they just leave?" she asked.

"It seems that the men get in debt to the bosses, and aren't allowed to leave until they've paid off their debt."

"What kind of debt?" she asked

"Food, whiskey, tobacco. The usual," he said. "Only these bosses are not usual. They've even threatened me, but so far I've been able to stay a step ahead."

"But they make plenty of money," she said.

"They do, but there is no law in the backwoods. I help as best I can, discourage men from going, but when the man doesn't speak good English, or can barely read and doesn't have a way to make a living, it offers wages and a place to live."

"I see," Annie Laura said, her stomach tightening, a queasy belly nearly getting the best of her here in the shadows of mid-afternoon. "Thank you kindly," she managed to say.

He only nodded.

She took the map and mounted her mare.

Was James caught in one of those camps, she wondered? And if he was, could he get out in time for his wedding, now less than a week away?

She put everything out of her mind other than this mission. Including the words her husband had spoken last night. She had promised to not look back. Had she kept her promise? She had no regrets about her decision, and that would have to do for now.

When she entered the piney woods, far from any towns or settlements, the horse smelled water long before Annie Laura saw it. Annie Laura drank from the refreshing stream, too, refilled her water tin, and nibbled on the dried biscuits and dried ham she'd packed in her saddlebag.

She heard the camp before she saw it, and the sound of axes chopping unremittingly, one after the other, like the throbbing of her heart. Something creaked, and she looked up to see the needles of an enormous pine quiver, and then, slowly begin its long journey to the ground, followed by the earth's resounding reverberation. Her horse shied, taking quick steps sideways into the palmetto-strewn underbrush, and Annie Laura saw a rattlesnake thick as a man's arm rush across the road, escaping the fall.

She calmed the horse and sat for a moment trying to decide which way she needed to go in order to find the camp.

"Ma'am?" The deep voice startled her.

She jerked in the saddle and turned to see a dark-skinned, red-shirted woodman holding a hand up to stop her forward progress.

"This ain't no place for a woman traveling alone," he said, his voice stern but kind.

"Who are you?" Annie Laura asked.

"I'm Brother Randall Joe Barnes," he said. "I'm a minister of the Lord."

Annie Laura noted his white teeth, neatly kept hair, clean pants, and polished black leather boots.

"I'm here looking for a relative. What's a preacher do around here?"

"I travel and minister to the men," he said.

"Do the bosses mind you being here?"

He looked at her, gauging her, it seemed. "It's a dangerous business," he offered.

"I heard," she said. She waited while he looked her over.

Seemingly satisfied that she posed no threat, he lowered his voice. "The bosses, they don't like meddlers. I tell them my goal is to calm down the men, make them think of their heavenly home, understand the pain here on earth is temporary, give them patience to bear it. They like that. Makes the men calm." He smiled. "Who are you here for?" he asked.

"I'm looking for James Stewart," she said.

"I'm sorry," he said, "I should have explained. I haven't been at this camp long enough to know the men by name. What's he look like?"

Annie's face grew hot. She hadn't actually met James. She tried to remember how Viola Lee had described him. "Taller than most, around six feet. Lanky. Tight, curly blonde hair. Big blue eyes. Full lips. Large nose. Uncharacteristically dark complexsion."

The man studied her. "Mulatto?" he asked.

Annie Laura caught her breath. She hadn't known that.

The minister did not miss her surprise. He nodded. "I know him," the minister said. "He's supposed to get married Saturday, but I'm not sure the boss is going to let him go."

"Why, he can't keep a free man here against his will," Annie Laura said.

The minister's face told her otherwise.

"The men call me Pastor Joe. I'm pleased to meet you. We'll tie your horse up here." He pointed to a skinny scrub oak closer to the road than the camp.

Annie Laura complied, left the horse with a feedbag, and followed Pastor Joe. The woods were filled with woe, the very trees seeming burdened, their heavy branches dipping low to the ground, and the single man they passed wore the grim expression of defeat.

"Are all the men here like that?" she asked Pastor Joe.

"Some of them been driven hard," he said.

"I can feel that," Annie Laura said.

This wasn't a prison camp, or a slave plantation. This was a work camp for men who had accepted jobs to cut timber, good-paying jobs that took them away from their kin but guaranteed a small savings so that they could buy land or a mule. She'd seen the posted notices, had heard the excitement of the men recruited to work for the company. She thought for a moment. She'd never heard a follow-up story on a single man.

They rounded a corner and the sight before her chilled her blood.

A man was tied to a large pine tree, welts and cuts all over his body, his neck lank, his chin bobbing against his chest. His body looked young, but his face was lined and he seemed folded into himself.

"Don't say anything, miss," Pastor Joe whispered, taking her arm and pulling her forward. "Avert your eyes."

"What's she doing here?" a tall, raw-boned man with black hair and beady black eyes asked, holding an oak limb in his hands, emerging to stand in front of Pastor Joe, blocking their view of the man tied to the tree.

"She's looking for her kin," Joe said, shrugging and smiling, lowering his gaze to the ground. "You know how ladies are, worried about they babies."

The man snorted. "I know about that. The snivelers write their mamas and beg to come home. Pansy boys, right, fellas?"

Annie Laura turned to see a lethargic group of men standing against the chinked pine log wall of the only structure in sight, watching. A few muffled "yeahs" was their response. They all studied the ground, never lifting their eyes to the boss.

Annie Laura tried not to respond, sensing that if she showed the horror she felt, she would be forced to leave. She felt she had happened upon some sort of savage tribal law. Had James suffered the same horrors as this poor man tied to the tree?

"What has that man done to deserve such treatment?" Annie Laura asked, trying to keep her voice as even as possible.

"Ma'am, we caught him stealing the earnings of some good men," the boss said, his chin high, his eyes narrow slits. "He ain't worth the ground he's standing on. Have to make an example of him so that all of these men here get what's coming to them. They work hard for their money, and they don't deserve to be cheated."

Annie Laura cast a glance at the men behind her. Their eyes were hooded, and not a single man nodded his agreement. She felt her skin tighten as if a bug had crawled over it.

The boss looked at the men. "That's enough fun for the day, now. All of you get back to work."

The men filed silently past, stealing a glance at her, but quickly averting their eyes when they came to the man tied to the tree.

"Now, what is it that I can help you with?" the boss asked, leering close to Annie Laura's face, his tobacco-stained teeth brown, his breath sour.

She took a step back and said, "James Stewart. I'm looking for James Stewart."

The man thought for a moment, shook his head. "Can't say I know a man by that name. You sure you got the right camp?"

"This was the camp I was given," she said.

"Well, ma'am," he said, tipping his greasy, broad-brimmed hat, "I'm afraid you've been given some mis-in-fo-mation."

Annie Laura watched his face, looked into his eyes. His shoulder did a little hitch, just like Jessie's did when he was lying, only Jessie usually lied to protect somebody else. This man, Annie Laura guessed, lied only to protect himself.

"Pastor, I'd appreciate it if you would escort our visitor right on out of here."

"Yes, sir," Pastor Joe said. "I'll do that."

The boss tipped his hat. "Ma'am," he said, turned on his heel, and strode out past the log building, following the men.

"Help me," the man tied to the tree whispered. "Help me."

Annie Laura hurried to his side, but was stayed by a brown hand clasping her arm.

"No," Pastor Joe said, pulling her back.

"James ran," the man croaked. "He made it. I didn't."

Chapter 11

Niggling at the back of Viola Lee's brain was the question *why*. Why was Walter Blakely her father? Surely her mother hadn't loved him? Why had her mother given her up for adoption? Why hadn't she been allowed to be raised in the family filled with love that she imagined her mother's to be? She would have loved being raised in a house full of younger sisters and brothers rather than in the deathly silence of her own house.

She was on her way to Ruth's house. Today, they planned to put the final touches on Ruth's dress for the wedding. Given all the chaos, Mary Scarlett had said no to a church wedding. Viola Lee was bitterly disappointed. Even though it would be in her mother's parlor, Viola Lee was glad she would have Ruth to stand beside her as her maid of honor.

"We'll make it fun, Viola Lee, don't you worry about that," Ruth had said, reassuring her. "And James will come home. I know it."

Viola Lee tried to believe her. Whether her heart was in this parlor wedding or not, she had to pretend all was well. She would go through the motions of wedding planning with Ruth and Mrs. Merritt, who had been planning her wedding for weeks.

The original food plans wouldn't change. Ruth's mother was making teacakes and homemade blueberry tarts from the sweet blueberry preserves she had put up the previous summer.

"Make them small, Mama," Ruth had said. "We don't want to wear blueberries down the front of our dresses."

"Nor do you want blue teeth for the wedding party!" Mrs. Merritt said, laughing. "I can't believe my little other daughter is getting married," she continued and hugged Viola Lee. "I know your dress will be the talk of the town."

Viola Lee nodded. "Mother has spent weeks on it. The bits I've seen have been beautiful, but she doesn't want me to see the whole thing until it is finished."

"Nobody sews like Mary Scarlett," Mrs. Merritt said, nodding her head approvingly. "And the time she spends on her creations. She should have been a fashion designer for some fancy house in London or Paris."

Viola Lee giggled at the notion of somber Mary Scarlett, dressed in her daily browns, a fashion designer.

All of these happy things she remembered as she walked up the front porch steps of the home that was nearly as familiar as her own. By the time she knocked on the door, her hope had partially returned. She was able to imagine her wedding.

A red-faced Ruth answered.

"What is wrong?" Viola Lee asked, pulling her friend to her and hugging her.

But Ruth pulled away, and in a falsely bright voice answered, "Nothing. Come on in."

Viola Lee walked in and the very atmosphere of the house felt different. Mrs. Merritt stood with her hand on the table, flicking crumbs into her other palm.

"Good morning, Viola Lee," she said, and there was something strained in her voice. Her smile was thin, her face a mask of worry.

"What happened?" Viola Lee asked.

"Nothing," Ruth said, brushing off her concern. "We're just weary of the heat. Mighty hot for April."

Viola Lee looked at her friend. The heat hadn't bothered her yesterday. Ruth's face was clean of everything but an engaging smile, and Viola Lee relaxed. The heat could get you down, that was for sure.

"It is hot. Every ceiling fan in the house is going at full speed," she said, looking up at the ceiling fan in Ruth's house and wondering why theirs weren't running yet. Like Viola Lee, Ruth's house had electricity and "newfangled fans."

Viola Lee followed Ruth into her room and Ruth shut the door securely behind them, in spite of the boxed-up heat.

But Viola Lee noticed that her house was not hot at all. In fact, the high ceilings and shade trees surrounding the house made it so that Ruth's house was cool, almost as cool as an early spring day.

Ruth's bridesmaid dress was hanging on the door of her walnut chifferobe. The white eyelet was trimmed in delicate pink embroidery at the neck and sleeves.

"It's beautiful!" Viola Lee said. "When did you finish it?"

Ruth was her own seamstress, as her mother was too busy with the duties of a farmer's wife to sew.

Ruth's face reddened. She looked down at the floor, picked up a stray white thread. "Yesterday morning. I was going to show it to you this morning."

"But instead, we had to watch Daddy shoot at that man."

Ruth nodded. She looked ashamed.

"It is embarrassing," Viola Lee said. "I am sorry you had to see it," she said, testing the waters. She needed Ruth there. Ruth made the entire thing feel like it was not real, like it was happening to someone else, and for right now, Viola Lee was pretty sure she needed it to be happening to someone else.

She wanted Ruth to jump up, hug her, and say, "Of course I would be there with you! Where else would I be?"

But instead, Ruth sat down on the bed and traced a circle on the white linen bedspread.

"I have some bad news," she said.

Fear gripped Viola Lee. A sinking sensation, like she was in a dream and falling, falling, falling. She knew what Ruth was going to say before she even said it.

A knock on the door. "Ruth? Viola Lee?" It was Mr. Merritt. What was he doing in the house at this time of day instead of out in the fields?

"Yes, sir," Ruth said obediently, though Viola Lee had not heard the question asked to which she was responding, "Yes, sir." It was as if this conversation was preplanned, and Ruth had taken her into the bedroom and closed the door in order to avoid it, but here it was in spite of her desire to leave it behind her.

"I need you girls to come out here. Your mother and I need to talk to you."

They filed out. Viola Lee was sick of feeling guilty for something she had not done. Her birth certificate read "illegitimate." She knew that. And because of that, some people had not wanted her to be the organist at the church, as if she were to be blamed for her birth.

But the pastor had fought for her, had said, "He who is without sin cast the first stone," to the busybody ladies who tried to block Viola Lee. And those same ladies tittered and chortled when Viola Lee had announced that she was marrying James Stewart, and then had shunned Viola Lee. She didn't understand it.

But the Merritts had been true friends. They were not close to Mary Scarlett, but they loved Viola Lee like she was their own, and Viola Lee knew this; she could feel it.

"Ruth will not be able to go to your wedding, Viola Lee. If it were up to me, I would take you to Panama City with James and secret you away there to start your lives away from the gossip of this town."

The lump in Viola Lee's throat did not allow her to speak. Why this? Why now?

"Walter Blakely is a known felon. His crimes are unmentionable, and I cannot allow my daughter anywhere he might be. Until he is safely behind bars, I fear he will continue to follow you and your family. I have to protect Ruth."

Viola Lee's face reddened. A wave of shame swept over her. Besides "illegitimate," did "criminal father" need to be stamped on her birth certificate as an additional note?

Her shame turned to fear. What if James Cornelius did not want to marry her? What if that was why he had disappeared? What if the circumstances of her birth, over which she had no control, had tainted not only the entire town against her, including her best friend's parents, but her fiancé as well?

She wasn't good enough for anyone.

But her fear smoldered into anger. She swallowed, her eyes narrowed, and she said, "To hell with all of you."

She walked out of the home where she thought she had felt unconditional love.

Chapter 12

Viola Lee knew what she had to do. She had far more to worry about than who was coming to her wedding. What she really had to worry about was whether or not there was going to be a wedding. If Walter Blakely's assertion that her mother was a whore was true, then her mother had been a prostitute, and the likelihood of James somehow being her misbegotten brother was a real possibility. She couldn't even allow herself to think about it.

It would take Viola Lee the entire day to walk the journey to Waterfall to find her birth mother. On a horse she could get there in half a day, visit with her mother, and be home by nightfall. She would need a horse. She would also need food and water.

In the kitchen, she packed her lunch. She cut the bread she'd made the day before and sliced ham from the pie-safe. She filled a jug with water and attached a string to it so she could tie it to her saddlebag. She wrapped the food in a cloth napkin and knotted the corners. She was ready.

Viola Lee hurried down the back stairs into the early morning sun, and headed to the barn where they still kept two horses and a cow, in spite of the fact John Sebring had a car. Cars could only take you so far. Most places you still needed a horse.

She saddled the gentle mare and led it past the shop side of the house. The horse snorted just as they walked past the open window of the shop. In less than a minute, Mary Scarlett's head popped out of the window. What was she doing in there before sunrise?

"Where are you going?" Mary Scarlett asked. Behind her, Viola Lee could see her wedding dress laid out on the sewing table.

"Ruth and I are going to see if we can find some pretty wildflowers for the wedding," Viola Lee said, her words as bright as she could muster. She prayed for forgiveness for the lie, and she prayed Ruth and her mother would stay far away from the dry goods store today.

"Be back in time to get supper cooking," Mary Scarlett said.

"Daddy said he would fry us up some fish and hushpuppies," Viola Lee said. Another lie. But she knew her daddy would cover for her if she got caught.

She mounted her horse and took the dirt road leading to Waterfall. She didn't know the exact location of her mother's farm, but the postmaster in Waterfall would know.

Viola Lee rode down the road that became eerily silent of people and filled with the sounds of the swamp. The road from Grassy Glade to Waterfall was long and desolate. She passed through the swamp and beyond the sand hills to where the Econfina forest crowded close in on both sides. The wild sounds frightened her, but she could not be afraid. She had to press on.

She rode until the sun rose high above her head, and there were no shadows. Her mouth was dry, but she pressed on. She did not pass a single person, not a single rider.

She rode until she was thirsty, and knew she would have to find a place for drinking water for the horse. She wiped her hair from her eyes, braided it, and stuffed it in an awkward bun to cool off her neck.

When the sun began making shadows behind her, and her fear had calmed, she had clarity of vision and thought. She was thankful for the father who had raised her and, in many ways, for Mary Scarlett. It seemed they had rescued her from a life of shame. They had given her nearly everything she had ever wanted. It was true that she had to do most of the housework and cooking, but Mary Scarlett was making the money that supported all of them. She didn't begrudge John Sebring his role. Though he didn't really make money, he kept them fed, and he was the joy in their home.

Caught up in her thoughts, she didn't hear the crackle of leaves, or even the whinny of a horse. She saw a well in front of an abandoned home.

She dismounted and tied the horse to a nearby tree. The wood around the well was crumbling, but the rope holding the dipping bucket was sturdy. She let down the bucket, imagining the sweet, cool taste before it even hit the water.

The well was narrow at the top, but she peered in and could see that a few feet down it widened dramatically, and she wondered at that, wondered why someone would have dug such a wide hole. But then she figured maybe they had tapped into an underground spring; maybe the well had gotten bigger of its own accord. The clay gave way to sand near the bottom; she could feel it against the sides of the bucket. She leaned down to look, holding tightly to the splintery wood frame. She did not want to fall in.

She laughed at the thought. She had never known anyone to fall in a well before, but she had heard of it happening to small children. Never anyone she knew, and never in Grassy Glade.

The wells there were too narrow and had to be aided by a pump.

But out here, there were springs all around. She wondered if this family found a spring beneath their well, why would they abandon their home?

And then she remembered. Indian raids. Families killed. Long ago, but recently enough that the surrounding towns had memories.

This place was haunted.

The sun was at her back, her shadow stretching long on the grassy patch in front of the well.

She peered down, and then the skin on the back of her neck prickled.

She lifted her head and saw not one but two shadows.

She looked behind her.

Walter Blakely.

The full stupidity of her situation hit her hard. She had chosen to come here alone, and this was the result.

"Are you lost, little girl?" he asked, his too sweet words dripping like poisoned candy.

She stiffened and moved away from the well; fear choked out thirst.

She looked around for an escape, for help. She was alone on a road halfway between Grassy Glade and Waterfall. She was in the middle of nowhere, in the front yard of a family that had been killed by Indians, a haunted place.

What was Walter Blakely doing here? Was this his bizarre attempt at trying to connect with his birth daughter? Did he mean to harm her? If so, why?

She decided to try to speak reasonably to him. "Why have you come after me after all of these years?"

He seemed startled by her question.

He studied her, took a deep breath, opened his mouth as if to speak. Closed it again.

Then, Walter Blakely did something she would never have expected in a million years.

He sat down beside the well and wept. "I'm going to hell," he moaned. "There is no hope for me. None. The pain I've caused. The havoc I've wrought. God is an angry God and I'm a sinner. Oh, God! Forgive me!" His voice rose in an angry bellow.

The violence of his outburst was more frightening than his sudden and unexpected appearance.

"I'm going to hell, but I'm not going alone!" His eyes bugged wide. He peered around like a blinded bull, his large head lolled, and then he fixed his eyes on her. Like a rabid animal, he sprang, snatched her up, whisked her away from the green grass, and dangled her over the well.

She screamed and kicked at the well's narrow sides. He held her by her hands and lowered her until she could see nothing but darkness. She stretched her legs out, positioned her rear against one side of the well and her feet against the other. She would not go down any deeper. He yanked her up, high enough to see the sky, and then dipped her down again, as if he were dipping a candle in soft wax.

She wedged herself tightly again, but this time her shoe dropped off her foot. There was a long pause before it splashed, and the splash made the water sound as if it were unfathomably deep. She stole a glance into the darkness beneath her, but there was nothing to see, only black nothingness.

She waited for him to jerk her out again, or force her down. She pushed hard against the side of the well with one bare foot and tried to inch her way up.

"Oh, Jesus!" he moaned, and he didn't seem to notice her movement. "We are coming, we are coming to see you!"

Viola Lee had no intention of going to see Jesus any time soon.

Walter Blakely yanked her up again, pulled her high. "Take one look, Annie, one last look. That's where we're a'going. We are going home, Annie. We are going home!"

"I'm not *Annie Laura*—I'm *Viola Lee*!" she screamed, but he didn't hear her. She didn't want to die. She wanted to go home, to her Daddy, to Mary Scarlett, to her bed with its clean white blanket.

"I know who you are," he said, looking at her with bloodshot eyes. "You are Satan's child, spawn of evil. Get thee behind me, Satan!"

He was a madman, a crazy man. She planted one foot on the top of the well, determined that it would stay there. He seemed not to notice as he was positioning himself to climb up onto the top of the well with her, readying himself for their leap, but she was not going down with him. His grasp on her hands was growing slippery. She slung her other foot over the well's side, losing her second shoe to the frightening darkness, and now both her feet were hanging on the outside of the well. If she could propel herself up and away from him, she might be able to grip tightly enough with her knees to give her the leverage she needed to tumble over the side and onto dry earth. She guessed he couldn't hold on to her and heave himself up the side of the well. She was ready. In a split second, he loosened his grip on her hands, she jerked away, teetered precipitously on the edge of the well, and propelled herself over. Viola Lee fell onto the green grass, pushed herself up, and without looking behind her, ran with all her might back to the tree, untied her horse, and leapt up onto the saddle, urging the mare forward.

Would he follow her?

When they reached the road, Viola Lee had to make a decision. Would she go home? Would she go back to her old life and try to forget about the nightmare she had just experienced? But the truth was, she couldn't go back to her old life. Not until she figured out if she and James could marry. And the only answer to that question lay to the north in the direction of Waterfall and away from home. She pulled the reluctant mare to the left, and kicked with all the strength in her legs until the road was a blur and the trees a green streak, and she and the mare raced against the wind.

Chapter 13

"There's only one road in and out of this camp," Pastor Joe said. "The rest of the camp is surrounded by alligator, water moccasin, and mosquito-infested swamp. Getting in and out of here? Only one man has survived so far."

Annie Laura had heard these words before. But if James was alive, she meant to find him.

"I know what you are thinking, ma'am. Ain't no way."

The beaten man, weak-voiced, spoke up again. "One way out," he said. "Indian trail. Chippewa man told us about it. The one who escaped."

Pastor Joe turned and studied the man. "No one else knows about it?"

"No, sir," the man said. "Chippewa only trusted me and James."

Annie Laura looked from one man to the other. "Tell me the way," she said.

"Be careful," he said. "Boss watching. Found me sleeping beneath a tree. James was scared of gators and slept in the tree. No one saw him. He grew up in the woods, knows how to make his way, knows how to be silent. The bloodhounds, they found me."

"Tell me the way," Annie Laura repeated, afraid the man would faint before he could speak.

"Three cypress trees, the mother, and two sisters mark the opening of the path. Near about a day's journey that way," he said and pointed. "You got a horse?"

Annie Laura nodded.

"He'll find the way for you."

The man pointed in the direction she was to go.

"Thank you," she said. "I'll tell your story."

"I'll be dead by then," he said. "But thank you. Could you tell Mama I love her? Edna Earle Johnson down in Wewahitchica."

"I'll find her," Annie Laura said. "What's your name, son?"

"Randall," he said. "Randall Johnson."

Annie Laura made her way to the boss.

"Excuse me, sir." She stopped a few feet away from him, planted her feet firmly, and waited for him to turn around.

"Something you need, ma'am?" the boss asked, smiling deferentially.

"I was just talking to the Woodmen of the World rep. He said there were a bunch of high-powered New Yorkers—reporters and attorneys, I think he said—on their way down here to find this camp. Can you imagine why they might want to come here?"

At first, the boss spread his chest and hooked his thumbs in his belt loops. He opened his mouth to speak, but then followed Annie's glance to the man tied to the tree.

Slowly, the boss's face blanched, his mouth gaped open, and his eyes darted around as if he were looking to see who might be listening. "Are you threatening me?" he asked, though his body position had changed some, his chest a little smaller. He unhooked a thumb and rubbed it against the tips of his fingers nervously.

She looked across at him, her grim face not matching the surprise in her voice. "Why would that be a threat?"

The boss didn't answer.

"Well," Annie Laura turned to leave, "I was just wondering. I told him I was headed here, and he said I might get to meet them."

"I ain't got nothing to hide," he called out after her.

"Well, good," she called over her shoulder.

She hoped her words to the boss had sufficiently frightened him into taking care of the man he'd beaten. She also hoped it would keep him from coming after her and James. She hoped she had bought at least enough time to find him. She prayed the Lord would forgive her for lying.

She'd read a couple of years ago in the Waterfall paper that a big lawsuit had been filed against the Jackson Lumber Company for peonage labor. The company had used brutality to force men to work in the forests of Alabama to supply logs for its Lockhart, Alabama, mill. She'd thought the lawsuit would have cleared up any more misconduct, but apparently it hadn't. She was sure the bosses were aware of the danger, however, and she guessed their bosses had warned them to beware of newspaper reporters and lawyers. Her words might at least put a stop to the brutalities for a few weeks until the boss figured out no newspaper reporters were coming.

She thanked the pastor and Randall.

Pastor Joe called after her. "I can come with you. You know they got the bloodhounds out after him."

"Might be best I go alone. You stay back here and take care of this man. I reckon the boss will let him down and make sure he's doctored soon enough." She smiled. She hadn't planned on the bloodhounds. She would figure something out. Right now, she had to find James.

She felt their eyes on her as she left. She turned and waved.

She heard the boss call out to the pastor, "Untie that man and help him to the mess hall."

"I reckon she done saved your life," she heard the pastor tell Randall.

"I hope mine is worth saving," the man responded, and then she was out of earshot.

Chapter 14

Annie Laura found her horse and looked for the path into the swamp. Randall Johnson's words rang in her ears: *Find three cypress trees—the mother and two sisters—the old Indian trail will take you through.*

Would she find James dead in a swampy grave? Torn up by the bloodhounds the boss had sent after him?

The men with the bloodhounds didn't know about the reporters and the possibility of scandal if their boss's cruelty was made public. Their mission was to bring James back to the camp, whatever the cost, and they would see Annie Laura as a mere impediment to their progress. She would have to watch herself.

She and the mare circled the camp twice before she saw the cypress trees.

They seemed to sit in the middle of a muddy slough. She could not see a way in that did not go through murky, moccasin-infested waters.

She urged the horse as close to the swamp as she dared, then let her have her head, praying that she would find a path that Annie Laura could not yet see. The horse stood, ears and nose quavering, for what seemed an eternity. Annie Laura felt the sweat bead and drip between her breasts. A wave of nausea caught her unaware, and she leaned over and retched. She wiped her mouth with the back of her hand, reached into her saddlebag, found a biscuit, ate it, and felt immediately better.

The horse picked its way forward along a small raised path in between two swamps, so narrow that Annie Laura had missed it. Pastor Joe had been right. Only a beast could find it. Annie Laura relaxed and trusted the mare to find the way.

She urged the mare forward, wanted to get ahead of the hounds, but the mare would not be hurried. Her walk was slow but steady, and Annie's skin prickled. Ahead and behind—indeed, all around—the swamp looked endless.

With no sign of humans before or behind, Annie Laura felt strangely alone. How had the bloodhounds missed this path? Or had they? Were they even now ahead of her, mauling James? She listened, but heard nothing, the swamp a shroud.

She prayed a little and saw the beauty of the afternoon shadows, noticed the spring flowers blooming even here, deep in the swamp. The leaves of the trees—not yet the brown and brittle of old age—were newly green and filled her with a feathery hope.

She retained this state of mind for what seemed like miles, but may only have been minutes. The singing of the birds lulled her, their late afternoon sounds punctuated by the call of a gator, the croaking of frogs, the sound of the breeze rustling through massive pines and cypress trees. The cool shade made her sleepy after the hot sun, and in spite of the danger around her, she dropped her chin and allowed herself to doze and dream for a moment.

Something awakened in her, a feeling of girlishness she'd not felt since before her first baby was born. Here, alone in the woods, she felt not terror but hope. The worries of the farm and her children seemed far away.

Here, she was on a mission, an adventure, maybe even a quest. She could not control it, and therefore, she relaxed into it. It was a blissful feeling and one she feared she could get quite used to. How lovely not to be in charge, not to be in control, not having to plan a meal, wipe a child's face, worry about insects in her crops, or too much rain rotting the young plants.

Here in these woods, she was something else entirely. A woman alone on a quest to save someone.

She liked the sound and feel of it.

It was the bloodhounds' moan that shattered her peace and startled her back into the world of men.

She jerked, and her mare did likewise; her ears perked, flickered in the direction of the sound. The mare stopped her forward trudge and waited.

Annie Laura trusted the mare to move forward when the time was right.

The bloodhounds bayed on the other side of the swamp far off to the east. The mare pushed on in her journey west, in the direction, Annie Laura prayed, of James.

She wondered why the bloodhounds had not found this path, and then realized that the men had probably guided them hard, not allowed them their heads, steering them out of the swamp where the hounds were certain to lose the fresh scent of man.

Because she had given the mare her head, the mare was simply heading in the direction of home.

"Look there!" she heard a man shout.

The sound was followed by the "clickety-click *bam*" of a shotgun.

Annie Laura tightened her grip on the mare's reins and urged her forward. She had been seen.

It wouldn't take long for the men to figure out the path. Soon, the bloodhounds would be hot on her trail.

"Come on," she urged the horse. She looked back across the swampy pool and saw the men scrambling around on the shore, giving the hounds their heads so that they could find the path she had followed.

Now she prayed that God would lead her to James, that he would be alive, and that she would be able to take him to safety before the hounds found them.

It would take the men a while longer than it had taken her. They were on foot. But the hounds would be here soon enough.

Annie Laura forced the mare to a reluctant trot. The way was uncertain, and the mare preferred to take her time, find her way.

Annie Laura squeezed the reins in her hands, but forced herself to trust the mare, and let her slow down to a cautious walk.

If she hadn't, she would have missed James.

He sat near the top of a great cypress tree. His bright red shirt drew her attention.

"Take your shirt off and throw it down here," she said.

He nodded and tossed the shirt down to Annie, who threw it deep in the swampy woods.

She wondered why he trusted her. He'd never seen her, he didn't know her. Was it because she was a woman? She didn't have time for thinking. They had to move.

"Now come on down on the opposite side of the tree, where I threw the shirt. Wade through the water," she said. "We can both ride on this here horse, but you need to climb up from the water."

He studied her for a moment.

"Come on," she said. "They're coming."

He climbed down from his safe spot in the tree and waded through the water.

Annie Laura led the mare toward the water. She balked. Sweat broke out on Annie's brow. She heard the hounds baying closer. She calmed herself, talked sweetly into the horse's ear, rubbed the side of her neck, and the horse took two grudging steps into the water.

It was enough. Straight from the swamp and leaving behind no trace of his scent other than the shirt thrown deep in the swampy woods, James threw himself over the horse. Annie Laura pulled him up and steadied him while he maneuvered his thin body to a sitting position in front of her.

She gave thanks for the mare's calm spirit and prayed the ruse would buy them time.

James turned, cleared his throat to speak, but Annie Laura shushed him with whispered words. "Don't you say a word until we are safely out of these woods and somewhere closer to civilized folks."

James nodded. The horse's hoof beats were masked by the baying of hounds in the distance.

The thick palmetto and pine brush closed in behind them like so many fans. They couldn't be seen unless the hounds were right on them, but the hounds did not rely on sight.

After a while, she heard the hounds stop, barking excitedly. They'd found the shirt. She prayed they'd hunt in the woods for a while before following after them, and for a while it seemed that would be the case.

The swamp was eerily quiet. Her ears burned trying to make out a sound that would alert her to their coming. Nothing. Silence. A bird twittered. A frog croaked. Then silence, the only sound James's labored breathing and the muffled plodding of the horse. Perhaps they had lost the trail! The ruse had worked.

The baying of a lone hound betrayed their position. James jumped, grunted. It drew closer, and she knew this hound had found them.

"You're going to have to hop down and climb another tree." But the trees closest to them were bare, dead cypress in the middle of the swamp. She urged the horse forward looking for a lush tree. There were none in sight.

Sweat broke out on her neck as the hound bayed, coming closer and closer. James was mute. She wanted to scream, *No!*

The path closed in on them. Annie Laura and James leaned down to avoid being swept off by the branches that guarded and canopied the path. James hugged the horse's neck, and Annie Laura clutched James's skinny back.

"Do you think you can climb this one?"

Just then, the mare's ears perked. Something heavy fell from the tree limb above them and hit the mare's hindquarters. The horse throttled forward in a fully panicked sprint.

The large black snake slid from the mare's back and onto the ground.

Annie Laura and James hung on, and the mare sprinted with a speed Annie Laura would never have guessed she possessed.

Chapter 15

Viola Lee thought of the anger in Annie Laura's eyes when Walter laid a hand on her arm back on the ferry. Annie Laura had stood between them like a mother cat defending her kittens. It made Viola Lee feel safe.

She imagined what Annie Laura would have done had she witnessed this scene.

The entire experience had been so frightening as to feel not quite real. If that was her father, did that mean she, too, might be crazy?

Walter Blakely was crazy and needed to be in a loony bin.

Thank goodness Annie Laura seemed right as rain. And, maybe, since she looked more like her mother than her father, she would take after her? She was short and blonde with Annie Laura's blue eyes. Hopefully, she also had Annie Laura's sanity.

The clay road to Waterfall was shaded with century oaks. The oaks grew closely together and kept the harsh sun from burning a hole in her uncovered head. She'd lost the gardening hat she'd grabbed on her way out of the house. No telling where along the road it lay. She'd been riding fast and furious and had just slowed the horse down to a walk. She didn't want to damage the gentle mare. She had plenty of time to think now that she was quite certain she wasn't being followed.

She needed to rethink her family connections. Her adoptive mother, Mary Scarlett, was Walter Blakely's brother. That made Mary Scarlett…her aunt? Would she have more sympathy for her brother or for her niece? Would she even believe that Walter had tried to kill her? Viola Lee knew John Sebring would believe it. Even though she wasn't even blood-related to him. That was a strange thought. The only other person who had showered her with unconditional love was not even related to her. Did he think on her as if she were his own? He had lost an infant daughter and his first wife in the Great Fire. She would have been only a year or so older than Viola Lee.

The Waterfall Post Office appeared on her right, the first building in the small town. She took her horse to the public trough and let her drink for a moment before tying her to the hitching post in front of the post office. Her legs felt weak after the long ride and she had to walk slowly. The line in the post office was long. The woman in front of her held a small boy by the hand. He turned and looked up at Viola Lee.

"Hi!" he said.

"Hi," Viola Lee replied.

"What's your name?"

"Viola Lee," she replied, smiling at the friendly child. His shirt was made from a flour sack, and his well-worn overalls had a neatly mended hole at the knee.

"Are you new in town?" he asked.

"No, just visiting."

"Who you visiting?" he asked.

"Annie Laura Seymour."

The woman turned around and gave her a friendly smile. Her dress was threadbare, and her shoes appeared to be two sizes too big, a man's brogans. "You kin?" she asked.

Viola Lee blushed. "Yes, a cousin."

"I've never seen you here before." Her tone wasn't prying. Just a matter-of-fact statement.

"I've never been here."

"You know how to get to her farm?"

"No, not really."

"Well, I can take you by. Her land's right next to our'n. You got a horse?"

"I do."

"Well, then, just follow us. This here line's way too long. I'll come back in the morning when the entire town isn't waiting on their mail."

Viola Lee smiled at her good luck.

The clay road narrowed to a trail, and the woman pointed and waved to a narrow lane to Viola Lee's left. She nodded her thanks and headed down the lane. She was finally here. Her heart filled to nearly bursting. She was going to see her, and tell her the entire sordid tale. She could just picture Annie Laura in a crisp white apron, serving cake to her sweet children. There would be a place at the table for Viola Lee, she felt certain.

The woman called back to her. "I don't know when she's a'going to be back to home. Sonny here said he saw her take off early this morning when he was out feeding the chickens."

Viola Lee's heart sank just as quickly as it had filled.

What should she do now? She looked up at the sky. She'd only given herself enough time to sit down and talk to her mother for an hour, no more.

Should she go on and try to meet some of her half-brothers and -sisters?

Fear gripped her. Did they even know she existed? But, yes, they had to. She had the handkerchief that Louise had made for her wedding day. That was it. She would go in and thank Louise for the hankie and then be on her way.

Something warned her this might not be such a great idea. But curiosity got the better of her. She wanted to see her mother's children, wanted to see if any of them looked like her. Maybe one of them would see her and mistake her for one of their very own sisters. The thought made her giddy. To have brothers and sisters. What must that be like?

A dog barked, and a man she had not seen turned to stare at her. He was leaning on a stick. He fixed her with his deep brown eyes.

"Hello," Viola Lee said in her brightest, most friendly voice. "I'm Viola Lee—"

"I know who you are," the man said gruffly. "What do you want?"

Viola Lee flushed. What did he mean he knew who she was?

"I was hoping to see my—Annie Laura Seymour," Viola Lee said, trying to recover her poise.

"Daddy?" a young woman came up behind him. She was dressed in a flour sack dress, too, neatly made, but faded. Her hair was the color of Viola Lee's, and she was tiny, just like Viola Lee.

Viola Lee smiled at her shyly, hoping for a friendly response.

"Get on out of here, Louise," the man said. "This ain't any business of yours."

The girl studied Viola Lee with a friendly gaze. "Don't you think we ought to ask her in for some water and refreshment?" she said. "It looks like she's come a long way."

"She ain't come that far, and she can go right back to where she came from," the man said. "Go on, now. Git," he said.

Viola Lee's face was hot, and tears smarted in her eyes.

She turned the horse around. *Illegitimate. Bastard child.* The words hummed in her ears like so many bees. She'd been treated just like this before; there were families in her town that would not let their children play with her.

Her best friend, Ruth, was one of the few children who could.

She turned the horse and rode blindly down the road, the tears coursing down her face. What right did this man have to humiliate and embarrass her? Who was he?

She let the horse take her back to the main road; she let the reins go slack. She was exhausted. Beyond exhausted. She wiped the tears from her face and untied the water jug from her saddle bag. She drank thirstily, wiped her mouth, and set her face toward home.

No use looking back. Her birth mother was gone and there was no one there who could or would help her.

She patted her horse's neck and spoke softly to her. "We'll just take our time walking on home," she whispered. "Maybe we'll meet Annie Laura on the road home. You never know."

She looked up at the road ahead of her. The town of Waterfall was off in the distance. Between her and the town it looked like someone was standing in the middle of the dirt trail waving at her.

Was it her mother who came home? Did she recognize her from this far away?

Her heart rose once again with the hope of being comforted by Annie Laura, the only person who would really understand her fear, a hope she'd nourished since leaving Walter Blakely.

But it wasn't her mother.

It was Louise, the girl in the flour sack dress.

Louise held something in her hand. Viola Lee pulled back on the reins. The obedient mare stopped, and Viola Lee reached down for the cloth-wrapped parcel.

"I thought you might be hungry," she said. "These here are biscuits I made this morning before Mama left. She took some on her trip stuffed with ham. I don't have any ham left. I'm sorry."

Viola Lee looked down at her face. Her words were kind, but there was anger in her face. Viola Lee climbed down off her horse and let it graze on the sweet spring greens on the side of the road.

"Thank you kindly," Viola Lee said, accepting the proffered gift. "These will taste mighty good, I know it. The trip home is a long one."

Louise nodded in agreement. She studied Viola Lee as if she were a plant that Louise was trying to decide was fit for her garden or not. She pressed her lips together as if holding words in she might say but couldn't, or wouldn't.

Viola Lee waited a few moments to give her a chance to speak. "What is it that you're wanting to say but can't?" she asked.

Louise looked surprised. "It ain't nothin'," she said.

This was not the meeting Viola Lee had imagined between herself and her sister. Louise didn't seem at all happy to meet her. In fact, while she seemed curious, she also seemed as if she resented Viola Lee's coming. Was it because of her father's anger?

"Why is your Papa so angry at me, and what happened to his foot?" She guessed the man was Louise's papa, though she couldn't be sure. He looked to be a rough sort.

"Papa's angry because his foot hurts and because Mama took off this morning on one of her 'harebrained missions.' That's what Papa calls them."

Viola Lee waited for an explanation. When one was not forth-coming, she said, "What kind of 'harebrained missions' does your mama go on?"

Louise squeezed her mouth, and Viola Lee saw that she wasn't just holding her words in. Tears leaked from the corner of one eye.

"You," she choked out.

"Me?" Viola Lee sputtered. As far as she knew, Annie Laura had only been on one "harebrained mission" to see her. "I've only seen her once and that was Saturday."

Louise's eyes widened. "You saw her?" she asked.

"Of course I saw her," she said, not meaning to sound rude. And then it occurred to her that Louise had said "missions." Not "mission."

"She doesn't go down to see you," she said. "She goes down to see about you. A man named John Sebring meets up with her and tells her all about how you are doing."

"That's my daddy," Viola Lee said. Though not my real daddy, she reminded herself.

"I think my papa is scared that Mama may go down to see you and never come back." The words were a challenge.

"Why in the world would he think that?" Viola Lee asked, genuinely surprised. Why would Annie Laura want to leave this life with her farm and all of her children and come to the mess in Grassy Glade?

But then she thought about the man who was Louise's papa, and Annie Laura's husband. Not at all what Viola Lee imagined. Why did Louise's papa look more like the town drunk than like the upstanding citizen she had imagined? She looked at Louise's well-worn flour sack dress and at her own finery—the Swiss lace peeking from the edge of her petticoat, the fine cotton of her blouse. And while she was barefoot now, having lost her shoes in the horror at the well, she had more pairs at home. She guessed Louise had only the shoes on her feet.

Viola Lee felt in her pocket for the handkerchief Louise had embroidered for her. The linen was fine and soft, and she wondered at the sacrifice. Louise had given her a fine gift, more precious because of her obvious sacrifice.

"Are you the one who made my lovely wedding handkerchief?"

Louise kicked the dirt at her feet, blushed and nodded.

"Well I thank you kindly. It's the most beautiful thing I've ever owned and a gift I will treasure always. I plan to carry it right along with my flowers on my wedding day." If she had a wedding day.

Louise smiled. "I like making beautiful things. I'm glad it pleases you." She made another hole in the dirt with the toe of her shoe.

Viola Lee waited a moment before she asked her next question. She didn't want to ruin the moment and she didn't want to be rude.

Louise looked up at her as if reading her thoughts. She waited for her to speak.

"You said your mama left this morning on a 'harebrained mission.' Do you know where she was going?"

"I don't. But my aunt does. Do you want me to find out?"

"No," Viola Lee said. "But thank you." There was no time. As it was, she would be lucky to make it home by dark, and she did not want to be alone in the dark with that crazy man on the loose. The crazy man who was also her birth father.

The thought sucked out all of her energy. She wished she had never known. She wished she could have lived her life believing that her father was some long-lost love of Annie Laura's. She wondered what other ridiculous notions she had cherished. Was her dream of a happy marriage with James just as ridiculous? She thought not. She couldn't control how other people lived. She couldn't even know or understand their lives. All she could do was give thanks for the people who loved her and try to recognize and cherish that love for what it was.

And start her own new life with James.

It was true that some townspeople saw Mary Scarlett as hard and mean, but she worked hard, and all of the money she made, she shared, and made their home as nice as possible. She spent hours sewing dresses and other finery for Viola Lee, and her heart told her that it wasn't all about showing off her daughter. It was because, in her own cranky way, she loved Viola Lee and put her heart and soul into the clothes she created for her. For whatever reason, Annie Laura had given Viola Lee away and started a new life here.

"I thank you again for the food," Viola Lee said. "I best be getting on. And if it makes you feel any better, there's nothing in Grassy Glade for your mama. She would never choose me over you."

The truth of the words nearly choked her. The truth was, Annie Laura had given Viola Lee away, probably because she couldn't bear to look at a baby whose father was Walter Blakely. She could only guess at how she came to be. Her mother's fear and anger when she had looked at Walter Blakely told her everything she needed to know.

Louise looked embarrassed. Viola Lee guessed Louise had never thought about it in that way, especially if her mother left them twice every year to check on her.

She didn't stay to find out. She kicked the horse. "Let's go home," she said. The horse wandered down the clay road and Viola Lee did not look back.

Chapter 16

Annie Laura and James hurtled through the flat swampland. Soon, the swamp turned to forest, and they pounded along a pine and palmetto path. Suddenly, the pine trees opened onto a neat farm perched upon a gently rolling hill. A farmer stood out in the middle of his field, a scene of such peace and normality that Annie Laura felt she was seeing a vision.

The farmer snatched off his cap as they hurtled toward him. With only a rickety split rail fence between them, Annie Laura hauled at the reins and the mare slid to a sudden stop. Propelled by the force of Annie Laura behind him, James flew over the mare's head and plopped on the ground, landing at the base of the fence in an undignified heap.

The farmer slapped his hat against his leg and chuckled, smile lines crinkling his sun-browned face.

Annie Laura hopped from the horse and kneeled beside James, who lay perfectly still.

The man hastily replaced his cap, slid under his split rail fence, and knelt beside the crumpled heap that was James. "Are you hurt, my friend?"

James looked up, his blue eyes wide with terror. It was then that Annie Laura saw the stripes on his face and chest, welts from a recent beating.

Annie Laura laid a gentle hand on James's arm. "You are safe," she said. "This man is just a farmer."

James closed his eyes and relaxed into the soft grassy earth. The boy, for that was all he was, lay on the ground as if all his vital energy had been expended making his way to freedom.

The farmer kneeled beside James and examined the stripes. He looked up at Annie, his face serious and sympathetic. His face reddened.

"I'm sorry for laughing," he said.

Annie Laura looked up at him and took his measure before speaking. The kindness in his eyes was genuine. "I probably would have laughed, too, and so would James, here, had we seen it happen."

The farmer looked grateful. "My name is Landers, and I am pleased to make your acquaintance." The farmer had a strange, stiff way of speaking.

"Mrs. Annie Laura Seymour, and likewise."

The farmer nodded respectfully.

James moaned. His eyes closed, he shuddered, and then lay motionless.

"He needs doctoring. Can you help us?" She put a hand on James's forehead, slick with sweat, but cold to the touch.

"I am not much good at doctoring the ill, but my wife has a gift for such things."

He sat unmoving, waiting, it seemed, for Annie's direction.

"Could you take him into your house?" Annie Laura looked back at the dark wood path, worrying they were followed.

"Yes," the man leaned down, slid his arms underneath James, set to lift him.

James' eyes bugged open, suddenly alert. He jerked away from the man, rolled himself into a tight ball like a roly-poly bug, covering his head with his arms.

The farmer squatted down, placed his hands on his knees, and studied James. "What happened to him?"

Annie Laura shook her head. She could only guess at the horrors James experienced.

She moved closer to James, careful not to touch him. "It's alright," she said softly. "This man aims to help you get strong so we can go see Viola Lee. I think she needs our help."

She waited a moment for the words to sink in. She touched his shoulder, he flinched, and she rubbed the smooth skin gently. He relaxed some, and made the effort to get up, but could not.

Annie Laura reached into her saddlebag for the water tin and held it to his lips.

He drank thirstily.

"Not too much, son," the farmer said, his voice soft, caressing, like he was talking to a spooked horse. "Not too fast. Otherwise you will not be able to keep it down."

James looked up at him.

"You need not fear me. I mean no harm. I would like to take you across the field to my house. There, my wife can take care of your wounds and help you become strong again."

James nodded, but his eyes registered renewed wariness.

James pushed himself up and fell. The farmer slowly reached a hand out. James took it, and the farmer cupped his elbow and helped him up.

He put his arm around James' waist, and James stiffened, but allowed it.

Annie Laura let out the breath she had been holding in a long, slow release. She took the mare's reins and followed the men.

They made their slow way around the newly planted field. A white wooden gate opened to reveal a neatly swept front yard. Annie Laura tied the horse to the fence and followed Landers and James up the stairs of the white clapboard house.

Annie Laura admired the generous wraparound front porch shaded by honeysuckle and jasmine trellises.

"You know about the lumber camp in the woods?"

The man's hooded expression told her he knew more than he wished to admit. "I've heard of it." He struggled to open the front door. "Elizabet?" he called.

"What is it, Landers?" Elizabet emerged from the back of the house, wiping her hands on her apron. "Oh!" she said when she saw Landers holding James. "The poor boy. What has happened to him?" she asked.

"He worked in the lumber camp," Landers said.

"Ach." The woman disappeared into the back of the house and reappeared, her arms filled with white linens.

Annie Laura guessed this was not the first man she had nursed back to health after working the lumber camp.

"They work the poor boys like beasts. Here, let him lie down here," Elizabet spread a clean white sheet on the elegant horsehair sofa, and lay another atop him. She lay the stack of linens on the wood floor and disappeared again. "Here, Landers. Do you mind filling this with clean water?" She handed him the pitcher for the wash bowl. She laid the bowl on the floor and looked up at Annie.

"Is he your son?"

"He is set to marry my daughter on Saturday. I needed to find him and talk to him."

The woman's brown eyes were soft on Annie's face. "We will get him strong enough to marry your daughter," she said. "He is young. He will be well soon."

Annie Laura did not know what compelled her to share more with the woman. Perhaps it was the compassion in her eyes. "My daughter is in trouble, I fear," she said. "I came for James so that he could help me protect her."

A look of understanding, and something else, flashed across Elizabet's face.

"She is not with child," Annie Laura said, her face growing hot.

Landers brought the water pitcher, and Elizabet filled the bowl with cool, clear well water. She dipped the rags into the water, squeezed them out, and handed one to Annie. They bathed James, washing him clean of the grime and sorrow of the lumber camp.

෨

The next morning, James was recovered enough to eat on his own. He had a lot to say.

"I worked hard to make the boss proud of me," James said. "I wanted to keep my job, bring money home to Viola Lee. But I was hungry all the time. They served us a couple of hard biscuits in the morning, a piece of bread smeared with bacon grease for lunch, and thin soup at night. I got so hungry I couldn't sleep.

"One day, I bought me a pack of stale soda crackers and a hunk of moldy cheese from the company store. I knew it would cost more than it should, but I had to eat or I wasn't going to be able to work much longer. I hadn't got my pay yet, and figured I could use some of it to pay for the food.

"I reminded Boss of my wedding. He just laughed.

"'You won't be going to no wedding this week,' he said. 'It will take you three to pay your debts.'

"'Debts?' I said. 'I only bought soda crackers and cheese.'

"'No, son,' Boss said. He smiled a mean smile at me. 'You got to pay for the shirt on your back and the brogans on your feet.'

"'But you said they were company issue,' I said.

"'They were company issue,' he said, squeezing his voice high, mimicking me like I was some little child. 'And it will take you another month to pay for them. Now you added some other stuff to your bill, and you're looking at six weeks.'

"I'm getting married,' I told him. Saturday."

"No, you ain't," he said. "You're cutting trees. Saturday.'"

"I looked at the evil in his eyes and I knew if I stayed any longer, I'd be a dead man. I listened to the talk about men escaping. I watched and waited for my time, and I run harder than I ever run before. I run to the woods, deep in the swamp. I reckoned I had a better chance of coming out alive dodging the gators and moccasins than the boss."

They sat at Elizabeth's table sipping coffee and eating ham biscuits and brown eggs, the yolks golden yellow and runny, perfect for dipping the feathery biscuits.

"But now," he said. "I got to tell Viola Lee I can't marry her. Not yet, anyways."

"Why not?" Annie Laura asked. Had he heard the rumor as well? Or worse, had he figured he didn't love her anymore? Annie Laura felt her stomach clench for her daughter. She had to ask him the question she'd come to ask. Was now the right time? Did she want to ask in front of strangers?

James's blue eyes shone clear, his dark face framed by tight blonde curls. "I got to clear my debts first."

Annie Laura breathed a sigh of relief. Her question could wait.

Landers said, "You have no debt. You owe that man nothing. You have paid by the sweat of your brow and the toil of your back."

"If that horrible man should try to come and find you," Elizabet said, "I would testify in court against him. I would," she said, wiping her brow with her apron.

"Do you think he would dare come after James?" Annie Laura asked.

"I do not believe so," Landers said. "Evil deeds are revealed in the light of day. Here, it is light. Evil men fear the light."

"But I owe the man money," James said. "He said I did. I don't want to be arrested and thrown into jail for debt."

Landers and Elizabet exchanged hopeless glances across the table.

Annie Laura nodded her head. "You are a good man, James. I am proud Viola Lee has found such a man. We will find a way to take care of your debt."

"I aim to pay back what I owe," James said with a stubborn set to his full lips.

"How, exactly, do you propose to return any money you might or might not owe to the man who calls himself your boss?" Landers asked. "Will you go back in the woods to do so?"

A look akin to panic flashed across James's face.

"Will you find someone willing to go back into the woods for you?" Landers asked.

He puffed his Meerschaum pipe patiently and studied James.

James ate the remainder of his meal in silence.

∂

They had stayed longer than she had meant to stay in the comfort and kindness of Elizabet's home. But Annie Laura had to wait until James was fit to travel. After watching him eat lunch enough for two on this day, she knew he was ready.

"I appreciate all of your help, ma'am. I would be a dead man if it weren't for you," James said. He walked alongside Annie's mare, guiding her through the rolling hills that signaled the end of the kind Farmer Landers's field. He had insisted on letting Annie Laura ride.

"I did it for Viola Lee," Annie Laura said. "And that's the truth of it." Was this the right time to ask James about his daddy? Annie Laura realized she was putting off the asking of it, scared of his answer.

"No harm," James said. "I'm glad she's loved. She's going to need love to get through these next weeks."

"What do you mean by that?" Annie Laura asked, pulling back on the reins gently to stop the horse. Obedient, the horse stopped and stood swishing flies with her tail, the gentle rustle the only sound in the noonday quiet.

"I can't marry her."

The heat rose on Annie's face, sure and certain. She leaned forward and patted the horse's neck to hide her sudden anger. "Why not?" she asked, keeping her voice measured and even. *What now?*

"At least not for a while. Maybe a long while. Maybe never."

With her back rigid, she peered into James's eyes. "Whatever do you mean by that?" she asked, and this time, her tone was neither measured nor kind. She wished to kick the sides of her horse and leave James in the woods where he came from. But first, she would find out why he dared speak these words.

"I cannot in good faith marry Viola Lee.Do you understand?" he looked up at Annie with pleading eyes.

"No. I don't." She sat on the horse and peered down at James, her eyes burning with anger. Was the anger justified? Or was the anger she felt something older, something more primitive? Was she angry at James, or was she angry at the man who had promised to love and honor her and, instead, had abandoned her for his lover of choice—alcohol—and forced her to raise her babies on her own? Another woman would have been much easier. The bottle never lost its allure.

"Come on." He pulled her horse forward.

But Annie Laura pulled back on the reins. "No."

"I have to get home," he said. "I have to talk to her. She is the only one who will understand."

"Try me," Annie Laura spoke through gritted teeth.

He looked up at her, shielded his eyes and recognized her anger.

"You are angry," his words filled with innocent surprise. "Why are you angry?"

Annie Laura wanted to say it was because he was a stupid, stupid man who had no earthly idea the power of his words. But he was a boy, really, not even seventeen. What did she expect? She took a deep breath, realizing she must speak to him like one of her children.

"I love my daughter," she said. "I don't want to see her hurt. I know her heart will be broken if you tell her that you can't marry her."

James looked at her like she had grown a third head. "It is nothing like that," he said, hurt filling his eyes. "I love Viola Lee. I just have to be able to support her. I thought I was working the lumber camp to bring home a big paycheck so we could start our lives. Instead, I'm bringing home debt. She deserves better than that."

Annie Laura couldn't help but smile at James. He loved Viola Lee. He only wanted to do what was right by her. What mother could resist that charm?

James was silent for a moment. He peered out over the fields and glanced back at the house. "I want something like this for Viola Lee," he said. "I want her to have a fine house and a big farm."

"If that is what she wants," Annie Laurasaid. "But what if Viola Lee wants to live in town? What if she wants you to run a store like her mama?"

"If that would make her happy, then that would be fine by me."

"You understand that Viola Lee wants you so badly, it doesn't matter to her how much money you do or do not have?"

"But it matters to me."

"Listen, James. Most of us start out with nothing when we marry. Nothing. But you, look at you! You can hunt and fish. You are a strong, smart man. You can work the lumber mill in Grassy Glade. They're hiring, I'm sure of it. And if that doesn't work out, there are two new mills over in Panama City that can't hire new workers fast enough."

"Really?" James's eyes glistened.

"Yes! You listen to me. Get on back to Grassy Glade. Get you a job at the mill. Then, find Viola Lee and tell her the good news."

"You pretty sure they'll hire me?"

"I couldn't be more sure."

"I'm mighty appreciative of your help. I can't thank you enough. And I can't wait to get back. I feel like I might have to run the whole way home."

"Well, then," Annie Laura chuckled, "what are we waiting for? Let's go ask her." She kicked the horse's sides gently. "Come on, gal, we've got miles to go."

They hurried along until the sun made shadows on the narrow road. They came to a crossroads, where she would go left for Waterfall, and he would turn right for Glassy Glade. Annie Laura knew now was the time.

"I've got something I must ask you before you go." Annie Laura took a deep breath.

He looked at her, his blue eyes serious.

"I need to know who your daddy is."

"Why are you asking?" Shame colored his face red.

Annie Laura felt a sinking in her heart. "I need to know."

He shook his head. "I don't know what you're lookin' for, but I reckon my daddy was my mama's husband. They was married a good two years afore I was born."

"I see."

"'Course I never got to ask my mama straight out. She died before I thought about things such as that."

What had Annie Laura expected? She felt cold fear and a rush of something else. Helplessness. Not a feeling she was used to, and it didn't set well with her.

"I got to go now," James said.

"Can you find your way from here?" Was she stalling?

"I will always be able to find Viola Lee. No matter where she is."

Annie Laura smiled. "I reckon I have to go now, too. I've got young'uns and a farm to tend to. They'll be needing me."

"You got a husband?"

"Yes."

"He run the farm?"

"No,. I do." Annie Laura set her face to the north and urged the mare to hurry home.

"Wait," James said, and she turned.

"What?"

"I wanted to thank you again."

"No need."

She watched him shift from one foot to the other. "Something else you wanted to say?"

He looked down on the ground, then back up at her. "I've never been with a woman." His face turned a bright red, and he looked back down at the ground as quickly as he had looked up.

Annie Laura was taken aback. Why was he sharing this? She felt embarrassed, but then realized he had no one else to walk with.

He waited for her answer, his face wide open and innocent.

She took a deep, steadying breath. "When the time comes, you'll know what to do."

He kicked the dirt up, then stomped it back down, frustration obvious. "I do not want to hurt her. She is so very small, delicate, like a wildflower."

Tears rose in Annie's throat, stung her eyes. "You won't hurt her. You're a good and kind man. You'll know what to do."

And she rode off before he could see the tears trickling down her face.

Had Leonard ever felt this way about her? It didn't matter. What mattered was for Annie Laura to make certain that her little girl, her firstborn child, could marry this man who loved her so much. *Please, Lord,* she prayed, *please let this marriage happen. If a miracle is in order, I pray that you would work one. She can't marry her brother, but please let her marry a man who treasures her so.*

Chapter 17

The shadows would reach home before Viola Lee did. Gradually the road transformed from hard clay to dirt and finally to soft white sand. Her feet were torn and bruised. But she was nearly home.

The gentle mare had tired several miles back. Viola Lee was forced to get off and walk beside the exhausted creature, unused to anything other than brief forays into the tiny town of Grassy Glade. She was old and certainly not accustomed to covering all these miles. Viola Lee refused to push her beyond her comfort. She had given the horse the remainder of her water.

When she heard the clopping of a horse's hooves behind her, her heart caught in her chest. What if Walter Blakely had followed her? What if right now, at this moment, he trotted up behind her and grabbed her and carried her off on his horse and dangled her over that well one more time? Only this time, what if he dropped her in?

She picked up speed and pulled the tired mare behind her, though her chest burned, and so severe was her thirst that she had no saliva left in her mouth. She looked back. The road was deserted. Had she imagined the sound? She turned her eyes toward home.

Her mission had been a miserable failure. She had discovered nothing about James' father. She had no idea where Annie Laura had gone. Would she be back before the wedding? And with Annie Laura gone, who could she go to for information about James's father?

Maybe James himself. Except that James wasn't here. Yet. Maybe he had come home while she was gone.

The comforting picture in her mind of James opening his arms and welcoming her home was overshadowed by the leering face of Walter Blakely peering out at her behind every tree. She shook her head, tried to shake away the vision. She had to get her mind off being followed or she would end up in the crazy house and would never make it safely home.

She forced herself to play the game she played sometimes when she could not go to sleep at night. In this game, she envisioned the wedding. Viola Lee envisioned herself walking into the parlor. She would walk up the porch steps, the door would stand open, the guests standing on either side, and at the end of the parlor would be James, his blue eyes dancing, waiting for her. She would smile shyly, and maybe he would cry.

She wouldn't think about who all was missing at the wedding—Ruth, her friends, the church itself. Nor would she think about the tiny group of people gathered, all friends and relatives of Mary Scarlett. Instead, she would think only of James.

What mattered was that she and James would be married. They would leave behind the horrible memories of Grassy Glade, shut off this place forever. They would move to the new Panama City, just across the bay, and she would never look back.

And in this new place she would create a new family. Ruth might join them someday wherever they lived. She imagined Ruth marrying a sweetheart and moving to Panama City. They would build houses side by side, and hang out their laundry together on clear mornings. They would laugh and talk about their husbands and later their children, and they would share all of their holidays together. She would forgive Mr. and Mrs. Merritt for not allowing Ruth to attend her wedding. But she wouldn't invite them to Christmas dinner.

She had walked a long way from home. Why had no one come looking for her? Not even her father? The shadows were gone now. Dusk grayed the sand road.

She could see light in the windows of the first house in Grassy Glade, but it was still a long way to her own house.

Once again, she heard the clopping of horse hooves a ways behind her. She turned to see who the rider was, but couldn't. It was too dark.

She forced herself to continue the game.

She and James would have four perfect children, and she would bake them cookies and he would build them a playhouse.

The hoof beats were closer now.

Their home would be the place where all the neighborhood children gathered. They would know the joy of family picnics and family Christmases, Santa Claus and the Easter Bunny; all the things that had been denied her, they would have. She would give them a childhood filled with magic.

The darkness was complete. She could barely see the road in front of her, was moving forward propelled by memory, her senses alert.

The horses hooves grew closer, gathered speed. If her water-depleted body could make tears, it would.

She moved to the edge of the road, afraid to move off the road, into the ravine beside it, afraid of what she might find. She had passed the swamp. What if there was a sleeping gator or snake? Rattlesnakes fed at night. She prayed that the darkness would hide her from Walter Blakely and she could stay safely on the edge of the road.

Just then, the moon shone a weak light on the road.

A single bullfrog sang, startling her. Others joined its chorus in loud rasping grunts and croaks, making it hard for her to hear anything else.

A horse and its rider throttled past her, and the frog chorus grew silent as if listening. When the lone bullfrog began the night song again, and his brothers joined him, Viola Lee continued her journey.

She plodded on, one foot in front of the other, her aching feet soothed by the cooling sand, the mare her silent companion.

Finally, the light from Mary Scarlett's window bathed the front yard in a yellow glow. She was home.

She lifted the latch on the iron gate and swung it open. It groaned and squeaked on its hinges. She stepped in the neatly swept front yard and turned to latch it. Something stirred on the front porch, the squeak of the rocking chair.

She looked up, but the chair was empty, rocking back and forth, as if someone had just left the chair and had walked inside.

She walked down the wooden walkway her father had built leading to the front steps. Almost there. She was thirsty, more thirsty than she had ever been, and the thought of the clear drinking water on the back porch beckoned her. She stumbled up the stairs and around the rocking chairs, walking the wraparound porch blindly.

She stepped around the potted geraniums on the narrow side porch, and finally made it to the back porch. She reached for the water dipper, laid her hand on the pump. But when she pushed down on the handle, she shrieked.

She had laid her hand on a hairy hand that was not her father's.

"Still thirsty, little girl?"

She backed away from the back porch pump into the screen door and screamed, "Daddy!"

"What is it?" John Sebring stood at the door, opened it, and Viola Lee fell into his arms.

"Seems like you'd keep a better eye out on that young'un of yours," Walter Blakely said.

John Sebring squinted through the screen door after closing it again. The darkness outside made it hard to see, but it was clear that he recognized the voice.

"What the hell are you doing back here?" John Sebring said.

"I brought your little girl back. And you ain't even a'going to thank me?"

"Walter?" Mary Scarlett came and stood beside John Sebring and looked out. She tried to open the screen door, but John Sebring had a firm grasp on the door handle.

"I was telling your husband here that I brought your little girl back. Don't look like anyone around here was any too worried, though. Didn't you even know she'd run away?"

"What?" Mary Scarlett trembled. "Don't talk foolishness."

"Well, I reckon you can take a look at those feet of hers and see that she hasn't been at no wedding party."

Mary Scarlett and John Sebring looked down at Viola Lee's bare feet, taking in the filthy, bloody cuts and scratches.

"What happened?" John Sebring asked, leaning down, gently examining her feet.

The pain in Viola Lee's chest threatened to turn into a full throated sob. She was an adult, now—almost a married woman, but she was afraid that if she tried to speak, she would bawl like a baby.

Walter Blakely filled in the gap. "I was minding my own business on my horse, just clip-clopping down the road, and what do I see? A little girl wandering down the road, all by herself. I tried to get her to come to me, but after what she saw you do to me with the gun and all, she was afeard of me."

Viola Lee found her voice. "You are a liar," she hissed. The sobs spilled out, and she couldn't catch her breath.

"Stubborn young'un you've raised. If I had her, I'da taken a belt to her more often than not," Blakely continued.

But John Sebring opened the screen door, nearly knocking him down, and said, "You come inside. I need to see you tell this story under the lights."

"I see where she got her stubborn streak," Blakely said and traipsed a boot full of mud into the house. "Anyway, like I was saying, I went after her on my horse and begged her to come back with me," Walter Blakely said. "She's probably thirsty."

Mary Scarlett pumped Viola Lee a glass of water at the kitchen sink, and Viola Lee drank thirstily, emptied the glass, and held it out for more.

"She was so thirsty when I found her, she near about fell in the well."

"He pushed me," Viola Lee said and choked on the water she was sucking down as quickly as Mary Scarlett could fill her glass.

"Here now," Walter Blakely said, reaching for Viola Lee. "Don't drink so fast."

She jerked away from him, spitting and coughing, her eyes watering.

John Sebring grabbed Blakely's filthy shirt collar and pulled him up to his tiptoes. John Sebring's six-foot-two frame towered menacingly over the smirking man. "If you ever put a hand on that child, I'll choke the life out of you," and he squeezed the collar until Blakely's smirk turned to red-faced panic.

"Let him be," Mary Scarlett said. "Until we hear the story."

John Sebring reluctantly let him go, pushing him off the porch as he did. Blakely sprawled in the gray dirt.

Viola Lee tried to talk, but water filled her throat. She gagged, and her face felt like it was on fire and her hands shook. When she could finally talk, her words came out in a hoarse, painful whisper. "He didn't bring me home," she said.

"How's that?" John Sebring asked her.

"She said I didn't bring her home, and she's right," Walter Blakely said, standing and wiping the dust from the seat of his pants. "I had to follow her to make sure she was safe. But I stayed far enough behind so she wouldn't know I was there. I followed her all the way here."

The thought that he had followed her all the way home made her skin crawl. The foolishness of her fevered run, the pain she endured with her bare feet and thirst, made her angry, angrier than she had ever been.

Viola Lee turned on Walter Blakely. "You are a liar," she said, venom replacing the water in her throat. She turned to face Mary Scarlett and John Sebring. They had to believe her. They couldn't possibly believe him. She squared her shoulders. Stood firmly on her sore, bare feet.

"He held me over a well," she said, her voice strong and even. "He threatened to drop me in."

"She's a pretty little liar, isn't she?" Walter said, shaking his head, reaching for the handrail.

But his voice wasn't as certain as it had been. He cleared his throat and changed his tone from slightly desperate to a mocking cynicism. "Has she always lied like this?" He put his foot on the first step.

"I've never known her to lie," John Sebring said. He picked up the gun he kept beside the back door to keep varmints away from his garden.

"Nor have I," said Mary Scarlett.

Blakely put a foot on the second step.

"You stay where you are," Mary Scarlett said.

John Sebring raised his gun.

They stood together, Mary Scarlett and John Sebring with Viola Lee between them. For the first time, Viola Lee felt a solid wall of family unity.

"Look," Viola Lee said, pointing to her torn and bloodied feet. "I lost both of my shoes in that well."

Mary Scarlett knelt down, ran a soft hand over Viola Lee's sore ankle, gently lifted her foot to examine the cuts through the filth.

She looked up at John Sebring, her lips pursed, anger making her eyes smolder.

John Sebring looked from Mary Scarlett to Walter Blakely. He cocked the gun and aimed it at Blakely. "Get out," he said, his voice menacingly soft. "Now."

Walter Blakely turned, picked his hat up from the dirt, slapped it against his leg, and muttered under his breath, "Lying little bitch."

"I'd like to kill you, I would," John Sebring said. He kept the gun trained on Blakely, who sauntered away.

Mary Scarlett led Viola Lee to the wooden table bench. Viola Lee sat down. Mary Scarlett warmed water on the wood stove, poured it in the china bowl. She took a soft linen towel, knelt down, laid a gentle hand on Viola Lee's filthy ankle, lifted it onto her clean white apron, and washed Viola Lee's feet.

Dirty rivulets of water dripped from her feet into Mary Scarlett's lap. "I'm sorry," Viola Lee said, and it was then that she saw the tears dripping from her mother's face, mingling with the warm water with which she washed her feet.

Chapter 18

Annie Laura reached home as the sky turned from orange to pink and the shadows disappeared from the road, replaced with light gray shadows. The whippoorwill sounded his plaintive call, and she was glad to be going towards the lantern alight in her kitchen window.

Louise had probably set the lantern. Her little girl was always on the lookout for ways to please her mama. She gave thanks for that relationship, was happy she had such a daughter. She prayed that Louise would have a daughter of her own one day who loved her mama like Louise did.

She rode the good and faithful mare down the side road to Aunt Martha's, stabled her, brushed her, and fed her. She was, she knew, avoiding home, avoiding Leonard. But she had to face it now rather than later. She gave the mare a final thank you pat on her withers, and climbed up the hill to home.

Leonard sat on the back porch, rocking alone.

"Leonard," she said, wanting to pass by him without stopping, go into the house, and gather up her babies.

She tried to brush past him, but he took her hand.

Fear coursed through her. What did he want now?

But when she looked into his face, what she saw was a mask of pain.

"I'm sorry," he said. "I mean it."

Something about the way he formed his words was different from the five hundred other times he had offered his apologies after being out drunk all night. Tonight seemed different.

"What changed?" Annie Laura asked, straightforward as always.

Leonard smiled. "You don't miss a beat, do you, missy?" he asked.

She smiled back. She wanted desperately to believe in the possibility of shared warmth, a moment like when they first married, before he started drinking. Her hope rose, as it always did, no matter how many times it was dashed.

"I mean it this time, Annie," he said.

"You have not answered my question," she said.

"I don't know, really," he said. "I've sat here thinking for two days with a pain in my foot that reaches clear to my head."

"Is it infected?"

"No. Not infected, just healing, and healing hurts. The pain from being shot wasn't nothing compared to how it hurt the next day."

She laughed, but her laughter was friendly, a response to his smile.

"I reckon I learned my lesson," he said.

"Did you?"

"You're hard, Annie."

"You've made me hard."

"Fair enough. I've treated you bad."

She was silent. He'd said this before.

"I'm going to change. I promise."

She wanted to roll her eyes.

"You've used me too many times, Leonard. I'm worn out. Time will tell."

"Fair enough."

She waited for him to say more, and when he didn't, she turned and went inside.

The house was neat as a pin. The ashes had been emptied from the woodstove, and the stovetop was sparkling clean. The table had been laid out for breakfast, and the dishes from supper had been washed, dried, and put away.

Louise sat in the rocking chair next to the window lantern darning a hole in her Sunday blouse. She looked up when she saw Annie Laura padding across the kitchen floor.

"Mama!" she said.

She jumped up and hugged her mama.

"All the others are in bed sleeping," Louise said.

"Good girl," Annie Laurasaid. "You've made the house sparkle. Thank you!"

"Oh, no, Mama," Louise said. "I didn't do any of that. Daddy did it all. He wouldn't let me help, said I'd worked too hard already in my life, and made me sit down last night and tonight while he cooked the supper and washed all the dishes."

"On that foot?"

"Yes, ma'am," Louise said. "He said the pain wasn't nothing, though after all the little ones went to bed he sat out on that back rocking chair and chewed on willow bark."

"Well, I'll be. I'll be."

"I'm glad you're home, Mama."

"Well, me, too, Louise girl. Me, too." And she meant it.

Chapter 19

The sizzle of bacon frying in the black iron pan woke Annie Laura early the next morning.

In the kitchen, Leonard stood on one foot, his knee propped up on a chair beside the stove, injured foot dangling. He had the griddle full of eggs that he turned one after the other, and she saw grits bubbling in the iron pot.

"None of the children are awake yet?" Annie Laura whispered.

"None," Leonard responded. "Not yet, anyway."

She saw the coffee had already been made, and the mottled blue enamel coffee pot sat on the kitchen table on a potholder in the starburst pattern. Mary had made it when she was first learning to quilt.

Annie Laura pulled a tin mug off the wood shelf to pour herself a cup. But Leonard stopped her, put a warm hand on her shoulder, and handed her a steaming tin mug already poured.

"Sit down and relax," Leonard said. "Tell me about your trip."

It felt strange not to be cooking, and Annie Laura didn't know what to do with her hands. Leonard finished cooking the bacon, laid everything out on a big platter, and spooned a plate for Annie Laura and one for himself.

He set a steaming plate before her. They fished clean forks out of the tin can in the middle of the table and bowed their heads.

"I thank you, Lord, for the blessings of this day," Leonard intoned. "Forgive us of our many sins, bless this food to our bodies and us to thy service. In your name we pray, Amen."

Annie Laura said her own silent thank you prayer and prayed that the change in Leonard would last. He seemed too good to be true. She had a feeling in the back of her head, something niggled. She'd heard that sometimes people turned good like this on their last days on earth. But that was an old wives' tale, she was certain, and she refused to take any stock in it. As far as she could see, he was healthy as a hog, no blood poisoning.

"I'm not much use to you out in the field, Annie girl, so I'm going to do what I can here in the house until my foot heals," he said.

Annie Laura swallowed her grits. She looked up at Leonard, but he was looking down at his plate like the words shamed him.

"That would be a big help to me," Annie Laura said softly.

A smile barely touched the corners of Leonard's mouth, and he nodded. "Well, good, then. You just tell me what needs to be done and I'll see to it."

Annie Laura went through the list of things in her mind that needed doing, crossed out the things that weren't entirely necessary, and split the difference. "I reckon wash needs to be done. Mary can help you with that, and the hanging out on the line. Start with the sheets. Looks like it's going to be a clear day, so they should dry fast enough for you to get a second set on the line. Do the children's underwear. They dry fast, and you can do their clothes tomorrow."

"What should I cook for dinner?" he asked, humbly.

Annie Laura studied his face and wondered if Aunt Martha hadn't doused him with some kind of herb that took all the fight out of him. She wondered if Aunt Martha had done so, why she hadn't done it sooner.

But that wasn't very grateful, she knew. And Annie Laura was grateful, very much so. But she didn't know this Leonard. It was like having a stranger in the house. An agreeable stranger, but a stranger nonetheless.

"Good morning, Mama." It was Jessie. He walked the long way around the table, avoiding Leonard.

Was that a pained look she saw flash across Leonard's face?

Annie Laura hugged Jessie to her, breathing in the sweet little boy smell of him. "Louise make you bathe yesterday?" she asked.

"Yes, ma'am." Jessie stuck his bottom lip out. "She said we needed to bathe every day now that it was so hot outside and we had the creek to dip in. Made me use soap."

Annie Laura laughed. "Well, good for Louise.Bedbugs don't go for clean boys."

"They don't?"

"You want to help me change the mattresses and wash the sheets today?" Leonard asked, his tone imploring.

Annie Laura looked at him, but Jessie leaned into Annie. "I think Mama needs me to help her with Dolly," and she had to admire how quickly his brain worked, to come up with such a plausible excuse.

"We've got more planting to do, don't we, Mama?"

Annie Laura smiled and squeezed him to her. "Yes, we do. We need to plant corn, and the north field needs plowing before we can do that."

"And sweet potatoes, too?"

"And sweet potatoes, too," she answered.

"You need to eat before you can do a man's work in the field," Leonard said.

Jessie shrank the minute Leonard spoke to him. He didn't want to take anything his daddy offered him. But the bacon smelled mighty good, and Annie Laura knew that bacon was Jessie's favorite.

Jessie's forehead wrinkled as if he were in deep thought. "I reckon you're right. A man can't work on an empty stomach, can he, Mama?"

"No, son. Not the kind of work we got to do."

Jessie nodded seriously. "We got some hard work ahead of us." He wasted no time eating the food his daddy put in front of him.

Leonard smiled a relieved smile, small, barely noticeable, but Annie Laura noted it, and her heart tugged a bit for Leonard.

How long would it take Jessie to trust Leonard? He was her most serious child. Slow to trust anyone, and the least likely to try new things. He was a little old man in a boy's body.

He was Annie Laura as a little boy.

Leonard studied Jessie with sad eyes. He'd lost his children. How long would it take him to win them back?

The other children stirred, and John Wesley padded into the room. He saw Annie Laura and started crying. He ran to her, his arms outstretched and his pajamas soaking wet.

"Sweet boy," she said. "Let's go out to the back porch and change those britches and put them to soak. We'll get you some clean ones, and you will feel so much better."

He clutched her around the neck, and she held him away from her so as not to soak her work dress. She took him out to the porch, unbuttoned his soaking pants, and wondered who had put him to bed in pants instead of his nightgown.

≈

Annie Laura, Louise, and Jessie came up from the fields for lunch when the sun got too hot to think.

They took turns washing their faces and hands in the cool pump water by the backyard garden.

"Mama?" Louise said. "Could I talk to you?"

"Jessie, would you mind running on up and getting to work in the garden?"

Annie Laura liked having a well-stocked kitchen garden. She grew collards, a few herbs, marigolds, tomatoes, peppers and other things that didn't do well in the field.

Jessie looked up at the garden, and Annie Laura knew he was checking to make certain Leonard wasn't around.

When he didn't see Leonard, he said, "Yes, ma'am," and trudged away, reluctant to leave Annie Laura's side.

"Mama, we had a visitor while you were gone," she said.

"Someone from the church?" Annie Laura asked.

"No," Louise said. "It was a girl." Louise's eyes filled with tears. "She was dressed in the most beautiful dress, and she was barefoot, and at first, I thought it was someone who had lost their way. But then Papa was mean to her, so I knew who she was."

Annie Laura frowned. What was the girl babbling about, and why would Leonard be mean to some barefoot girl dressed in a pretty dress?

And then the sickening realization hit her. "Tell me exactly what happened," she said.

"I was helping Papa walk. He wanted to see how far he could walk on the bad foot. He said a wise woman had told him a long time ago that the more you walk around when you're injured, the quicker you heal. He was walking a little in front of me. I saw him stop, and then I heard him tell the girl to go away. By the time I could see her, he had already been rude."

She stopped speaking and searched Annie Laura's face. Annie Laura knew her face was probably the white of the sand in Grassy Glade. "Go on," she said kindly.

"I ran back to the house to grab her some biscuits. She looked hungry and tired and sad."

"That was real sweet, Louise," Annie Laura said.

"I chased her down and gave them to her. She was looking for you. She said that she saw you Saturday, that you had talked. Are you moving away, Mama?" Louise asked in a burst of tears.

Annie Laura hugged Louise to her. "I would never leave you," she said. "Not until the day you marry and you choose to leave me."

"Why did you go see her?" she asked.

"It was time," Annie Laura said. "I had some things I needed to tell her. I still do. But something happened while I was up there. And there are some things that still need seeing to."

"But you'll come back?" Louse asked.

"Always," Annie Laura said.

They moved into the cool house. The high ceilings caught the heat of the day, and the big porch overhang all the way around the house kept the interior cool.

They ate fried chicken. Leonard insisted on the rich fare—he'd fried it up himself. "Nothing is too good for my family," he said. "I'm going to buy another mule. With two, I can help you. We can farm twice as much land."

His boastful words made Annie Laura's heart lurch.

"I want to take my babies down to the beach in Panama City," Leonard said. "I've heard the water is blue as a spring, and clear as a drop of rain. They say the sand is so white you'd think it was sugar, and the sky the blue of a robin's egg."

His eyes shone, and the children watched him warily.

Annie Laura wanted to warn him to take it easy, to slow down, to not try to win the children back with big promises, but take his time, earn their trust, and then, once the trust was earned, give them a treat. She didn't feel right about using treats to earn trust. It wasn't the lesson she wanted her children to learn. Some stranger could give them candy someday, and she didn't want them to trust treats over people. She wanted them to be able to look a stranger in the face and say, "No, thank you," until the stranger became a friend and had earned trust.

Leonard looked over at Annie Laura and said, "Not anytime soon, though. Too cold right now. We'll wait till first of June when all the planting is done, the crops are growing, and we do the first weeding. We'll go to the beach as a treat for the weeding. Fair enough?" His eyes sought Annie's.

She smiled in spite of herself. "Fair enough," she said. She decided not to mention Viola Lee for now. She had some things to sort out in her mind. Namely, how she was going to figure out who James' father was.

Chapter 20

It was while she plowed that Annie Laura had a thought that made her drop the plow handles and leave the mule in the middle of the field.

She strode toward the house, untying her apron strings.

"Mama?" Jessie called. "Mama!" He ran after her. "Mama, what's wrong? Is your stomach all a jumble?"

Annie Laura turned to her child and laughed. "I'm not headed to the outhouse, son. I'm headed to Mary's."

"You got a headache?"

"You might say that. I got some business I got to tend to. You reckon you can plow a straight row next to the ones I plowed?"

Jessie pushed his chest out and rose as tall as he could.

"Why, yes, ma'am!" His eyes glowed with pride. "I'll have the whole field plowed in just a jiffy."

"You won't need to do the whole field," she said. "I'll be back after you've finished...let me see..."

She stared back at the long rows, looked up at the morning sun, and did some calculations. "I reckon you can do five rows and then be looking for me to bring you some water and take over the plow."

"Yes, ma'am." He reached up to the plow handles. He gripped them tight. "Gid-up, Dolly." The patient mule ambled forward.

The plow whirred through the smooth black dirt. This area of the field was the least troubled by pine roots and stones. Jessie would be fine long enough for Annie Laura to go take care of her business.

She ran across the field and down the hill leading to Aunt Martha and Mary's house.

She smelled the sweet potatoes before she reached the front porch. She climbed the wooden steps and knocked on the door. She heard footsteps, the door opened, and Aunt Martha greeted her.

"Well, knock me down with a feather," Aunt Martha said. "What are you doing here in the middle of the day? Didn't I just watch you walk by plowing the north field?" Aunt Martha pointed to the line of oak trees that marked off the north field.

"Yes, ma'am," Annie Laura said.

"Are you ailing?" Martha asked.

"You aren't losing the baby growing inside you, are you?" It was Mary's voice, and though Annie Laura could not see inside the dark cabin, she imagined Mary sitting in front of the fire, patiently turning the sweet potatoes.

Aunt Martha invited her in and offered her a chair by the fire.

"If you don't mind," Annie Laura said, "I'd love to take a seat here at the table so I can keep an eye out on my Jessie."

"Suit yourself," Mary grumbled.

Aunt Martha laughed. "I reckon she's hot, sister. She's been out working the fields." Aunt Martha dipped some cool water out of the water bucket, and Annie Laura took it gladly.

Annie Laura looked out the window, squinted her eyes a bit until she saw Jessie.

Aunt Martha followed Annie's gaze. "You let that little old squirt of a boy push the plow?"

"Just for a little bit," Annie Laura said. "Just long enough for me to run over here and visit for a minute."

Aunt Martha eyed Annie Laura more closely. "Huh," she said and filled her pipe.

"I've never known her to visit us in the middle of the day, have you, sister?" Mary asked.

"That's a fact," Aunt Martha said. She tapped the tobacco down into her pipe and sucked on the stem for a bit. She didn't light it.

Annie Laura drank the water thirstily. "That's good water," she said brightly. "You must have the deepest, sweetest well in these parts."

"So they say," Mary said. "So they say."

"How are your sweet potatoes growing this year?" Annie Laura asked.

"Well," Aunt Martha said. She clutched her pipe and moved it from her mouth to her lap. "That ain't what you're here for. What is it that you've come here to ask? Are you ailing?"

"You ain't aiming to ask for a potion to get rid of that baby, are you?" Mary asked, her voice hoarse and wet. She cleared her throat and spit into the fire. The spit sizzled, and the foul smell of burnt snuff filled the room.

"Why, no, ma'am," Annie Laura said, horrified. "I would never do such a thing. I love my babies." Annie Laura stood. "I need to go check on Jessie." She was shaken, wondered if her coming here was a mistake.

"No need for you to take on so," Aunt Martha said. "Speak plain. What did you come here for? Now don't get your feelings hurt. You know we are always happy to see you, always glad when any of you drops in for a visit. The Lord knows it gets mighty quiet and lonely in here with just the two of us, but your face don't usually show up until the sun has long set and the children are put to bed. Is it Leonard? Is he set on drinkin' his life away still?"

"Oh, no, ma'am," Annie Laura said. "Leonard is sweet as a lamb. He's been minding the house, cooking, cleaning, doing the wash. The house was shiny spotless when I got home."

"Did you find out what you went to discover on your journey?" Aunt Martha asked.

"No, ma'am."

"And that's why you're here? It came to you all of a sudden that Mary here might be able to answer your question?"

Annie Laura looked at Aunt Martha, her eyes narrowed. "You already thought of it," she said, her tone accusing.

Aunt Martha said nothing, but the look on her face was smug.

"If you knew that Mary was the person I needed to ask, then why did you let me go running off looking for the answer in the wrong place?" Annie Laura asked.

"It didn't seem to do you no harm," Aunt Martha said. She put the pipe in her mouth and lighted it, striking the match off the bottom of her brogan. She took a contented puff, closed her eyes with a dreamy look on her face, then opened them again, blew out smoke rings, and watched them rise to the ceiling. Her eyes cut to Annie. "Look at all the good it did you, missy," she said. "You look happy, like you figured something out."

Annie Laura had to laugh and shake her head. "So you sent me on a fool's errand because it would do me some good?"

"You needed to get away from those young'uns. You needed a break. Leonard needed to see all you did. He needed to see what the house looked like without you. He needed to miss you some, see the error of his ways. It came at a good time."

How could Annie Laura argue with that?

"No, enough about that. Go on ahead and ask Sister your question."

"But didn't you already ask her, since you knew?" Annie Laura asked.

"No, I'm not one to go messing in someone else's business."

Annie Laura raised her eyebrows and Aunt Martha laughed. "Unless, of course, I'm set to heal something that needs healing."

Annie Laura shook her head.

"So ask," Aunt Martha said.

It was harder than Annie Laura had imagined. She hadn't planned how she would ask, and to ask the question meant reminding herself of the great horror in her life, the horror she would rather forget.

But she had to do this. For Viola Lee.

"Mary," she said. Her mouth grew suddenly dry. She took a sip of the water in the cool tin cup, swallowed, and tried again. "Mary, I need to ask you some questions."

Mary rose from her place by the fire and walked slowly, painfully, over to the table, sat next to Aunt Martha, across from Annie. The arthritis that gnarled her hands and stooped her back made walking difficult.

"There was a man, lived over Marianna way a long time ago. Came from Waterfall but married a Marianna woman." The lump that rose in Annie's throat made it hard for her to speak. Annie Laura blinked her eyes, hard. She wanted to wipe away the pain, wanted to forget what had happened, but she had to recall the memory to get what she needed from Mary.

Aunt Martha and Mary sat perfectly still, listening, absorbing her pain. The kindness in their eyes, the compassion, the love, made the story easier for Annie Laura to conjure.

Her mouth was dry again and she swallowed again, trying to moisten it. "He fathered my Viola Lee," she said. She paused because of the tightness in her throat, the hard lump of pain. "I think he probably fathered more children." She paused and swallowed again. "In the same way."

"The rapist," Mary said. "I delivered a few of his babies. Poor, poor girls. And now he's raped a girl up in Dothan, and a lawyer good enough to allow him to be released on bail before he stands trial. Now, how you s'pose he pulled that off?"

"Friends in high places, I reckon," Aunt Martha answered. "That and I'm not sure rape is considered a real crime in some courtrooms." And then she prodded her sister. "Do you remember the names of the girls whose babies you delivered?"

Mary closed her eyes. "The first one was a boy. Fine, squalling thing, came out easy as you please, though the girl was young, too young to be having a baby. I expected it to take longer, but it didn't. Her hips, you see, were wide. She pushed the baby out and wouldn't look at him. Her mother took the baby, wrapped him up, and held him. I finished cleaning the girl up, and left. I had another call, you see. A woman you know. That sweet friend of yours, died in the fire with her baby soon after."

Annie Laura nodded. She knew Mary had delivered John Sebring and Maggie's baby girl. Grief washed over her anew. Maggie had been her dearest friend.

"The next one was yours, and it was not an easy birth. But she came and you took her and nursed her and loved her."

Annie Laura tried not to think about the day Viola Lee had been wrestled from her arms.

"Next one was another boy. Over Marianna way."

"Who was the mother?" Annie Laura asked, leaning forward, brow furrowed, hoping against hope that the answer was not what she feared.

"Hadley Stewart," Mary said.

Annie Laura gasped. *So it was true. James was Viola Lee's half-brother. She couldn't marry him.* A flood of grief washed over Annie. The grief mixed with anger and she slammed her fists down on the table, upsetting the water cup. It poured off the wood table and spilled over onto the floor.

Mary and Aunt Martha sat watching it calmly, as if they had expected this very thing to happen.

"I'm sorry," Annie Laura said. She wiped the water up with the hem of her skirt. "I thank you," she said, and walked out of the door and back to the field.

She walked as if sleeping, and she didn't remember taking the plow handles from Jessie nor setting him to work picking up sticks and stones on the next row. She didn't remember plowing the field through lunch, in spite of Jessie's pleas for her to stop, take a break, eat something.

She didn't remember Leonard coming out to the field, forcing her hands off the plow, holding her. She didn't remember struggling and crying against him. She didn't remember beating his chest, though the bruises were the evidence early the next morning when she awoke to find him shirtless cooking her breakfast.

"I'm sorry," he said, his blue eyes wide with concern. "I didn't get the clothes hung out in time yesterday to have a clean shirt. Forgive me for going shirtless. Mama would backhand me if I ever tried coming to the table in such disarray."

Annie Laura nodded. She saw the mottled blue bruises the size of her fists. He looked down where she was looking.

"It's nothing," he said. "Nothing that I didn't deserve."

She gasped. "No," she said. "It wasn't you."

She stood, placed her hands on his chest. She ran her hands over the smooth, muscled lines, ran her hands down his shoulders, over the muscles in his arms, his forearms, stopped at his hands, laid her hands over them.

"I love you," she said. "I always will."

A tear brightened the corner of his eye. He struck it away as if it embarrassed him, as if refusing to engage in the dramatics that had characterized his previous dry spells. "It's different this time, Annie," he said. "I promise."

He drew her to him, and she smelled the clean smell of his chest, ran her hands over his smooth brown skin, clutched him in an embrace she wished would never end.

Chapter 21

A knock on the back door broke their embrace.

"Annie Laura?"

"It's your mother," Annie Laura said.

"What is she doing up so early?" Leonard asked. He returned to the stove, smiling.

He had a wonderful smile.

Annie Laura knew Mary to be a night owl, staying up until the wee hours of the morning and sleeping until nearly noon.

She said it was because that's the way babies got born. "Did you ever know any babies to be born first thing in the morning?" she asked.

Annie Laura opened the door and led her into the kitchen where Leonard stood over the stove, flipping the bacon in the cast-iron skillet.

"You get into a boxing match with Jack Johnson?" Mary asked, pointing to the bruises on his chest.

"Naw," Leonard said.

"Huh," she said and turned to Annie, who was looking guiltily down at her coffee cup. Mary smiled a half smile and sat across from her.

"There's more," Mary said. "I remembered something in the middle of the night. Had to wait till you all woke up before I could tell it."

"More?" Annie Laura asked, her face bright red.

"Children," Mary said. "Hadley Stewart had two boys and a girl. She died when the girl was born. She already had the fever, pushed that baby out, and they died together."

"Is James the firstborn or second-born?" Annie Laura asked.

"I don't know," Mary said. "I don't stay for the naming."

"What happened to Hadley Blair's children?" Annie Laura said.

"Jack Stewart, her husband, lived for another couple of years, best as I recall. After that, the children went to stay with Jane Dykes. She raised them on up, according to Sister."

"How did Aunt Martha know?" Annie Laura asked, *and why didn't she tell me?*

"She's been doing some asking," Mary said. "Church ladies, you know. Quilting circle. Wednesday nights. They talk a lot, and Aunt Martha went last night."

Annie Laura nodded. "Did you learn anything useful?" Shame burned her face.

"They didn't know which one of Hadley Stewart's children was the rape baby. Seems like she kept it hid and Jack Stewart raised them all like his own until he passed. Can't say the same for Hadley's mama and daddy. They had plenty of money and wouldn't take the children in. Sent them to live with Jane, who barely had two cents to her name. But she took them in and raised them and loved them like her own."

"Can I talk with her?"

"You can, but she won't say. Ladies said if anybody even tried to mention it, sweet Jane made a face that would have scared a panther away."

"Good for her," Annie Laura said.

It was good to know that the family Viola Lee was marrying into was made up of good, kind folks. It was good to know that even after she knew the circumstances of Viola Lee's birth, she would love her anyway.

"The rape baby had a birthmark," Mary said. "I remember them, those birthmarks. Tells me which baby is which since I don't get names. I name them by their birthmark. That baby's name was Cornflower."

Annie Laura laughed, surprised. "Cornflower?"

"You got something I could write with?" Mary asked.

Annie Laura scrambled for paper, found a copy of the *Waterfall Banner*, most of its margins already filled with writing of one sort or another. The children learning their letters, Annie Laura marking down the date she planted the first sweet potatoes.

She handed a clean margin to Mary and a stub of a square pencil.

Mary drew a dark center and encircled it with a series of fine petals.

"Why Cornflower?" Annie Laura asked.

"It was a tiny mark, size of a button, dark red, but he was a blue baby so I named him Cornflower."

"Where was the mark?" Annie Lauraasked.

"In the middle of his back."

"Would you recognize it if you saw it?"

"On a grown man?" Mary asked. "Yes, I would." She smiled. "Sometimes I see birthmarks that I recognize on children, and I know that I birthed that baby and it lived. Makes me feel good."

"There would be a lot fewer people in these parts without you, Mama," Leonard said. "You've been delivering babies since I remember."

"I delivered you myself," Mary said and laughed. "You gave me a hard time then, and haven't let up since."

Leonard smiled.

Annie Laura tapped the table. "We have to figure this out before Saturday," she said. "Viola Lee can't marry her brother."

Leonard beat the spatula against the side of the iron frying pan, and Annie Laura jumped at the harsh sound.

Louise came in from the bedroom, fully dressed.

Annie Laura drew in her breath. "Did we wake you up?" She hoped that Louise had slept through this conversation.

"Not really," Louise said. "I was already awake."

"Have you been eavesdropping?" Leonard asked, his voice angry.

"It is fine, Leonard," Annie Laurasaid. "She has to find out at some time. Eat your breakfast, child. You and I have a lot of work to do in the field today. And then you and I and Mary are going to take a trip to Grassy Glade. We have some business to attend to there."

∂

"I was twenty-two," Annie Laura said.

"You don't have to tell me this," Louise said.

"You've heard just enough to worry," Annie Laura said.

Louise reached down and pushed a sweet potato slip into the freshly plowed soil.

"I was working in the deep woods, clearing my land."

"You were alone?" Louise asked, pushing her hair from her eyes.

"Mama had just passed away, Papa was mourning, and the girls were too small to help. And I was working out my anger at Papa for giving up after Mama died."

Louise pulled another slip from her commodious apron pocket and pushed it into the soil. "You sure we're past any freezes?" she asked.

"Good Friday is tomorrow."

She continued, "I was lost in my thoughts and didn't hear him. After he attacked me, I went home. I told Papa what had happened. Papa said he would kill him. Instead, Papa killed himself."

Louise dropped the potato slip from her hand. It fell to the ground, bright green against the dark soil.

"Oh, Mama," Louise said. "That's so sad. I'm so sorry."

"I wasn't sad," Annie Laura said, closing her eyes and pressing her lips together. "I was angry. Angry as a mad bull. My papa was a coward. He killed himself and left me to fend for myself, my sisters, and the baby I didn't realize was growing in my belly."

Louise recovered the dropped slip and planted it, patting the soil around it a little longer than necessary.

"I think I would have been mad, too," Louise said thoughtfully.

"The Bible tells us in our anger not to sin," Annie Laura said. Her voice faltered.

Louise looked up at her, her brow furrowed. "You didn't sin," she said. "Your papa and that horrible man sinned."

"I haven't told you the whole story," Annie Laura said. "Come on, I think I'm going to need to sit down for this one."

She led Louise down to the creek that divided her property from her neighbor's. They sat under the shade of the old oak tree.

"After Papa died, and my baby was born, the sheriff took our land. All of it. My sisters and I were paupers."

"How could he do such a thing?" Louise asked. "Your daddy had paid for that land."

"Yes," Annie Laura said, "but the sheriff was sly. Papa had not made a will. The sheriff posted the land as unclaimed. He gave thirty days for it to be claimed, then he held an auction and bought it himself for a giveaway price. It wasn't the first time he'd done it."

"But why didn't you go get your land?" Louise asked.

"He posted the notice the week Viola Lee was born," she said. "I was in bed for three weeks after. By the time I knew what had happened, the land was gone."

"And that's when you met and married Daddy? Did he make you give up your baby before he would marry you? Was that your sin?" Louise asked. "If that's what happened, then it was Daddy's sin and not yours."

"No," Annie Laura said. "That's not what happened. Your daddy was not at fault."

Annie Laura gripped her skirt and squeezed as if the wadded-up fabric could give her strength.

"This here farmland that you are sitting on, all but the house we live in and the land behind that belongs to Mary and Aunt Martha. All this land you are sitting on is blood land."

"What do you mean 'blood land'?"

Annie Laura looked out over the spread of farmland that had nourished her family for nearly two decades.

"There was a married couple couldn't have any children. They were related to the sheriff and the man who attacked me. Money changed hands. Court documents were erased. I got my land. They got my baby. That's the end of it."

Annie Laura stood and walked away. She picked up her own bag of potato slips and began planting. The tender shoots looked so vulnerable in the massive soil mounds. It would take plenty of water and sunshine for them to grow. Deep in the soil, they would send down shoots, and those shoots would grow thick and round, hidden by the green vegetation and the dark soil. Come November, she and the children would harvest the sweet tubers, dig them up from their caves, expose them to the light. At first, they would be bitter, but after sitting for a few weeks, they would sweeten and be ready for the table.

She would never forgive herself for trading her baby for this land.

But maybe, just maybe, Louise would forgive her for all the time she spent away from home doing what she could to make sure Viola Lee had some small chance at happiness. Maybe now she could see that Annie Laura owed it to Viola Lee.

Louise and Annie Laura worked silently through the rest of the day and late into the night to finish planting the sweet potatoes. All of the children helped—some planted, others held lanterns, and still others brought food and drink.

Lying in bed that night, Leonard turned to Annie. "Girl," he said, "I know you are dog tired, but I got some things I got to say to you."

Annie Laura wished they would wait until morning. She could barely keep her eyes open. The day had been hot, the work and conversation had been grueling, and the bath on the back porch by the light of the moon had sent her into a dreamy state, one she did not wish to be jarred from.

"I am listening," she murmured, though she turned away from Leonard, and his words became a lullaby and soon she was asleep.

He shook her awake. "Sit up," he said. "I need to say this to you. It is a burden on my heart and needs saying."

She sat up slowly, wishing to curse him, but at the same time, there was something in his voice, something plaintive, something real.

"I know you have a lot of love for Viola Lee," Leonard said. "But after you straighten this out, you need to leave her alone."

Annie Laura narrowed her eyes. He was jealous. "She is my child, Leonard," she said. "After all these years, I have finally gotten the chance to speak to her, to see her, to know her. Why would you deny me that pleasure?"

"I know, Annie. I know," he said, and the compassion in his words made her stop and listen. "I know you love her, and she must know that. I know that you long to make up for lost time. If you could have it your way, she would build a house right next door."

She had thought that very thought. How had he known?

"We all long to have our children, to keep them with us, forever. But that's not the way of things. Our job is to raise our children and equip them with enough wisdom, knowledge, and strength to make it on their own. We have to push them from the nest so they will make their own way."

"I know there is wisdom in your words. But Viola Lee is different. I missed out on fifteen of her nearly sixteen, years. I only got her for a few months," and Annie Laura cried, the pain in her chest squeezing and squeezing until the tears squeezed from her eyes, and she cried again. Sobs broke from her that she hadn't known were there.

Leonard hugged her to him, pulled her in close, muffled the sobs in his chest, stroked her hair, stroked her back, murmured incoherent syllables that soothed her like her mother and grandmother had soothed her those many years ago.

"Listen," he said. "I know this is hard. If I could do it, I would give you all those years back. I would fight for you to be able to keep that baby, and we would have raised her like our own. But you know and I know that we did everything we could to get Viola Lee back, but we didn't have the money or the pull to make it happen. We've had to live with that. *I've* had to live with that...."

And there was something in Leonard's voice, something that caught. "I failed you early on, Annie, failed you at the one thing you wanted more than anything, to get your baby back. And with every baby we've had, I've prayed that this one would make you forget that first one. And when none of them did, I beat myself up over and over again. I couldn't face you."

"And that's why you drank so hard."

"I don't know," he said. "I just know that what I wanted was to please you and what happened was I couldn't, and it has hung over my head all these years. If I had been a better man, I would have gotten Viola Lee back for you."

His voice choked and, once again, he batted away a tear, angry that his emotions got in the way of his explanations.

Her heart filled her chest and she hugged Leonard.

"No, wait, I'm not finished yet," he said. "You have got to let her go, Annie. You have to. Just as I do. I have to let go of the fact that the one thing I wanted to do for you I could not do. I have to make peace with myself and with you over that, because if I don't, I won't be able to live with myself or you. I'm begging you to do the same. Let her go."

"Do you mean let her go forever?"

"No," he said. "I don't mean forever. I mean let her live her life. Plan something—I don't know, maybe plan to meet her every year, once a year on some special day. You'll both know that is when you will see each other, and you won't be fighting yourself every day for trying to figure out how much time you ought to give to her. You have a family full of babies who need you."

"But so does she," Annie Laura said.

"Viola Lee has a mother and a father. And while Mary Scarlett is not the woman I would choose for a wife, she loves Viola Lee from all I can see and hear."

Annie Laura looked at Leonard through new eyes. Every year for the past fourteen, Leonard had made fishing trips to Anderson, Florida. She had never understood why, exactly, he did it. She had thought it was to go drinking with his buddies. He always brought back fresh fish, but he always came back besotted and spent at least a day in bed getting over it, the stink of stale liquor emanating from his skin and filling the bedroom and house with it.

"Have you been checking on Viola Lee all these years, without telling me?" she asked.

"I just wanted to make sure she was taken good care of," Leonard said. "The child has worked hard all of her life, but she has been happy," he said. "She has had a sober father," he said, and put his face in his hands.

"You get to start over," Annie Laura reminded him. "With your children," she said. "You are here with them."

Leonard sat up and nodded. "Thank you," he said.

His embrace was soft that night. Their lovemaking took on the sweet, gentle rhythms she remembered from their first years, back before his drinking was bad, back before he was so angry.

She forgave him.

Chapter 22

Saturday morning dawned bright and clear, a perfect April day. The weather was cool, not cold, and the humidity was barely noticeable. Viola Lee awoke to the sound of birds singing. She smiled listening to them.

Until she remembered what day it was.

Her wedding day.

Only there was no groom. John Sebring had gone in search of James, had gone to the lumber camp where he was employed. He had found nothing, and no one willing to talk. It was as if James Stewart had never worked there.

She turned back over and buried her head in her pillow. She heard a tapping on the tin roof; more than likely it was a confused woodpecker. She put another pillow on top of her head and tried drowning out the sound but it was no use. The darn thing kept tapping; each tap sounded like the ringing of a bell. She grew still for a moment and allowed herself to count with the tapping. And then she heard it. A knocking on her window. She bolted upright in her bed.

She jumped out of bed and ran across the rag rug and onto the wood floor, opened her window, and looked around.

"James?" she called.

No one. She thought she saw movement beneath the window. A blonde head. She leaned out the window.

"Ruth?"

"I'm sorry," Ruth said, her face tear-streaked. "It's not James, it's only me."

"Oh, Ruth!" Viola Lee said and climbed out of the window. She hugged her friend.

Ruth hugged her back, and then looked at her. "You are so beautiful, Viola Lee. It's your wedding day! I had to be here with you!"

"James isn't here. Didn't your parents forbid you?" It would do her heart good to know that Ruth's parents had changed their minds. She needed people who loved her this day.

Ruth poked out her bottom lip. "They said I couldn't come to your wedding. They didn't say I couldn't come to your house before the wedding," she said.

Viola Lee tried to hide her disappointment, tried to make Ruth feel good about the kindness she extended by simply being here. It was hard.

"It doesn't matter anyway," Viola Lee said, and felt her throat grow sore and tears sting at the back of her eyelids. "I don't think James is coming."

"Of course he's coming," Ruth said. "It's not easy getting from that logging camp all the way to Grassy Glade. You know how it is."

"Daddy went looking for him," Viola Lee said. "He wasn't to be found."

Ruth shook her head. "There are so many logging camps, Viola Lee. How do you know he didn't skip out and find one that paid him more money? He probably worked right up until the last minute so that he could make plenty of money for you."

Was this a possibility? It wasn't like James had signed a contract or anything. Perhaps he could have found a better offer somewhere else, and maybe that's why the bosses didn't tell John Sebring. They didn't want to lose all their workers to a higher-paying camp. The thought relieved her as nothing else had.

"Are you going to take a honeymoon trip?" Ruth asked.

Viola Lee blushed. It seemed possible again. "We talked about going to Panama City and spending the night," she said.

"Where are you going to live?" Ruth asked.

"I'm not sure," Viola Lee said. "I thought we would have a day or two before the wedding to figure it all out. He's been gone three months, and three months ago it didn't seem like something we needed to worry a lot about," she mused.

"No, I don't imagine it did," Ruth agreed. "Just think. In three months, you could be pregnant!"

Viola Lee blushed and laughed. She hoped it was true.

But then another thought crossed her mind. Even if James did show up, would it matter?

"The things you say, Ruth." The thought made her so sad, so afraid. To think that in a year she could be holding her own baby. There was nothing she wanted more than to make her own happy family. But what if it wasn't possible? What if James was her brother?

Where was James? Why wasn't he here to dispel the frightening rumor?

"He'll show up, Viola Lee. I know he will. The wedding is set for seven this evening. He'll be here."

Viola Lee nodded. "I hope you are right."

"I would love to see your dress all finished," Ruth said.

"Well, come on in," Viola Lee said. After all, what could it hurt to pretend all was well?

They linked arms and walked around the house and up the front steps.

"Well, look at what the cat drug in, will you?" John Sebring smiled indulgently at the two girls. He seemed not to be the least bit worried about James.

He took a close look at Viola Lee, noticing her nightgown. "Did you spend the night outside?"

"No," she laughed. "Ruth showed up at my window and I jumped down to see her."

"Don't you let your mother see you outside like that. She'll have a hissy fit."

Viola Lee knew he was right. She and Ruth tiptoed into the house. Mary Scarlett was back in the kitchen. She could see her walking back and forth, preparing herself for the new day in the shop.

The store would not be closed. Not even on her wedding day. It would, however, close early. Viola Lee was disappointed. She had hoped, after their reconciliation, that maybe Mary had changed— that maybe she, Viola Lee, might be more important to her than the store, but it didn't seem to be the case.

She wondered what it would have been like with her real mother on her wedding day.

They reached her bedroom, opened the door. It squeaked on its hinges.

"That you, Viola Lee?" Mary Scarlett called.

"Yes, ma'am."

"Well, good," her mother said. "I didn't think you would ever wake up. I've cooked you some breakfast." She came around the corner and saw Ruth. "Well, good morning," she said, and looked puzzled.

The girls giggled.

"Would you like to join us for breakfast?" Mary Scarlett asked. Her eyes narrowed some and Viola Lee wondered if she was thinking about the fact that Ruth's parents weren't allowing her to come to the wedding. "I've cooked some sausage and eggs, and the biscuits should be ready in a minute."

If the girls were surprised at this turn of events, of Mary Scarlett cooking them breakfast, they didn't show it.

"You got any of your blueberry preserves?" Ruth asked with a big smile on her face.

Viola Lee suspected she knew the answer. It was the only thing that Mary Scarlett enjoyed doing in the kitchen. She loved blueberry preserves, and she methodically canned them every spring and into the summer as long as the blueberry bushes in the backyard produced.

Mary Scarlett beamed. "Yes, as a matter of fact I do," she said. "But I'm on my last few jars. Hope we have a nice big crop of blueberries this year!"

"Me, too," Ruth said.

They sat down at the table, and John Sebring joined them. It gave Viola Lee a warm feeling to have everyone gathered around the table on this, her day. She prayed James would come.

Chapter 23

"Annie!" Leonard called. "Wait!"

"Mama," Louise said, "it's Daddy."

Annie Laura turned from her perch on the wagon's front seat, and sure enough, Leonard rode Dolly, who lumbered slowly towards them. *What now?* she wondered. Had he changed his mind? Did he wish to go with them? That wouldn't do at all. Too many bars and temptations in Grassy Glade, what with the sawmill booming.

"Whoa, girl," Mary said, pulled back on the reins, and stopped the horse and the wagon.

Leonard strolled up, a big smile on his face. "Annie, girl," he said, "I've got some news. Remember Gegirl Johnson?"

"I remember him," Annie Laura pressed her mouth until her lips into a thin line. Gegirl Johnson was a sharecropper on the southern portion of Annie's land. His daddy died when he was seven, and he and his sister and mother sharecropped.

Or sat on the land. They'd not had a crop that produced since the daddy died. He had been a hardworking man. Gegirl, now twenty, was lazy. That was the only way Annie Laura could describe him. She had let them stay on as sharecroppers though there had been no crops shared. She felt bad for the mother and daughter. But even when Annie Laura knew Gegirl made money off the land letting it out for grazing, Annie Laura didn't do anything about it. She was blessed, she had plenty, and besides, she didn't have time to go to the courthouse, file a petition, and go back for the many hours it would take for the court to decide in her favor or not. Her experience with the court system in the past had not been pleasant, so she let it go.

"I know him," Annie Laura repeated. Of course Leonard knew she knew him. She waited to see what Leonard's real question might be.

"I seen him driving a car."

"A car? Is he driving for somebody?"

"No," Leonard said, working the muscle in his cheek. "Word around town is that he bought the car with profits from letting the land out to graze."

Cold anger burned through Annie. She had hoped he'd bought much needed food and clothes for his mama and sister.

"And I gave them a mule," she said. "A long time ago. I knew they couldn't farm without one."

"And there was only you working the land," Leonard finished for her. "I'm sorry, Annie. I should have been helping you."

"Words are cheap, son," Mary quipped. "Actions speak loud."

"Yes, ma'am," Leonard said, and he studied the ground. "But I aim to do right by you now, Annie. I aim to go get that mule back and work our land right alongside of you."

Hope floated up in her and choked her. She nodded, afraid that to say anything would break the spell. Afraid to admit how badly she wanted exactly this thing to happen, afraid that her desire would jinx the happening of it.

"Aren't you going to say anything, Mama?" Louise's gentle voice gave her courage.

She swallowed. "I would like that, Leonard."

Mary broke in. "But you take care. That Gegirl is a loose cannon. Has been since he was a little thing. I've seen him turn and rage on folks. When he was little, he shot his baby sister because he was mad at his mama. He missed, but I was there to see it. It was right after his daddy died, and he was just a little tyke. I thought then it was just grief and rage of a child who didn't know any better. But he kept right on acting that way well into his adulthood. It's a wonder he hasn't killed a'body."

Annie Laura nodded. "I've heard things like that about him." She wondered if that was why she had left the family alone. She just didn't want to deal with them. She knew that no matter what she did with them, it would turn into a big mess, so she might as well just leave well enough alone.

But with a man, a partner, someone who could come alongside her and help her fight her battles?

Life stretched out in front of her, lighted up like a sunny May day. Just like today. She shielded her eyes and looked over the land, *her* land. Hers and Leonard's. As far as the eye could see—north, south, east, and west—the land was theirs. Of course the tree line hid where their land ended, but that was okay, too. *Their* land. She drew in a deep breath of clean air and joy.

"I'm going to get the mule back, Annie. I'll be waiting for you when you get home."

She nodded, her throat full, too full of emotion to speak.

Leonard tipped his hat to her, his face filled with love.

He walked away.

"I think he means it this time, Mama," Louise said. "I think he's quit his drinking. I think he is going to be good."

Annie Laura smiled and hugged Louise close to her. "I think so, too."

She looked over at Mary who studied Leonard as he disappeared down the dirt road.

"I don't have a good feeling about this," Mary said. She made a tiny hole with her thumb and forefinger, looked through it with one eye, squeezed the other one shut. She'd broken her glasses and had to make do. She stared long and hard. "No," she said, shaking her head. "Don't feel good about this a'tall. Leonard is not even armed."

"Armed? Why would he need to be armed?"

"I told you," Mary said, "Gegirl Street is crazy."

"Call him back, Mama," Louise said. "Call him back!"

"He won't come," Mary said. "He's set on it."

"Daddy!" Louise called. She scrambled from the wagon, hit the clay road, slid, yanked up her skirts, and ran after her daddy.

He turned back, smiled a puzzled smile. "What's the fire you got light'n your butt, girl?" he asked, laughing.

"Daddy, don't go," Louise said.

"Girl, what are you so worried about?"

"Mary said Gegirl Street is crazy. Said he shot his sister."

Leonard laughed, reached down, and stroked her head gently. "Girl, you know Gegirl Street ain't one bit crazier than me."

"Daddy!" she said, and now her voice rose, nearly hysterical. "They said he shot his sister with a gun."

"I've heard that," he said, "but he wasn't nothing but a tiny tyke back then. Now you go on and stop worrying about your daddy. You've worried enough about me to last a lifetime."

"But Mary Louise said. "She said she had a bad feeling about this."

Leonard's smile disappeared. He shaded his eyes and looked down the road to Annie Laura and Mary.

"Is that a fact?" Leonard asked.

Louise nodded.

"Well," Leonard said, "I'll just have to be extra careful, then, won't I?"

"You don't even have a gun, Daddy," Louise said.

Leonard laughed at this. "It's not a war, girl, like what might be going on a'way over across the ocean! I'm just going over to have a neighborly chat and get back what's your mama's. Now get along with you. You are holding up the mission."

Louise stood and watched him stride away. He turned. "I love you, girl. Don't you ever forget that, do you hear me?"

"I won't, Daddy," Louise choked out. "I love you, too."

Worry came over Annie Laura like a pall. Leonard had never uttered those words aloud to any of his children, and only once to her.

Last night.

She looked at Mary who had fallen silent, brooding.

Annie Laura watched him disappear into the distance, swallowed by massive oak trees reaching down to him with mossy fingers.

Chapter 24

After breakfast, Viola Lee refused to allow herself to look down the road. She would not watch for James to arrive. She would trust that he was coming and leave it at that.

The ceiling fans creaked their protest against the morning heat. Viola Lee and Ruth refilled the pitcher and bowl at the washstand in her room, and set to arranging Viola Lee's hair.

Viola Lee sat in front of her dressing table and looked at herself in the mirror. The face was serious, round, her blue eyes wide with anticipation. Sadness bowed her lips.

"You better turn that frown upside down," Ruth said, touching her cheek lightly. Viola Lee took Ruth's hand.

"I have to believe he is coming, Ruth."

Ruth looked at her with a smile that was genuine. "Of course he is coming. We would have heard otherwise. Bad news travels quickly."

Viola Lee nodded. "I'm going to believe you." She tried not to think about the fact that there were still several hours between now and the wedding, hours that could be peppered with bad news.

"We are going to pretend like he's here," Ruth said. She brushed Viola Lee's hair out. It fell in fine, soft curls down her back.

Viola Lee closed her eyes and allowed herself to relax under her friend's ministrations.

A knock at the door, and Mary Scarlett came in. She held a lovely bit of embroidered silk gossamer in her hand, bunched at the top by a sprig of greenery. She spread the veil out on the bed, and left the room to return with three roses in a vase.

"We will wait until the last possible moment to attach the roses," she said. "The leaves will stay green until tomorrow. The roses may fade."

Ruth nodded, and Viola Lee stood, ran her hands over the fine silk festooned with delicate white embroidery.

"Oh, Mama! It's the most beautiful veil I've ever seen! I didn't know you had made me one!"

"I have to have some surprises," Mary Scarlett said. "And besides, I did not want you looking at it with moping eyes telling me what you wanted embroidered where. I wanted this one to be my own creation, as beautiful as you."

She walked out before Viola Lee could thank her properly, and Ruth said, "I think she is crying!"

Mary Scarlett never cried. In fact, while she could count the times she had seen John Sebring cry on one hand, the hand she held up with her mother's tears was empty.

"I think she is going to miss you," Ruth said.

Viola Lee wondered if she would miss Mary Scarlett. She decided she would. She imagined she would miss her a whole lot more when she got away from her.

"Let's check and see how it looks on your head," Ruth said, "before we actually do your hair, so that we'll know how to fix it."

They placed the lovely veil carefully on Viola Lee's head. A warm breeze blew in the window, lifting the veil, and sunbeams danced on the glimmering, undulating wave.

"It's a magic veil," Ruth exuded. "I think the fairies have come to visit you!"

Viola Lee giggled her response, because Ruth was right. The fabric was iridescent magic.

Just then, the metal gate creaked.

Viola Lee's eyes widened. "Do you think that was the wind?" she asked, all of her senses alert.

"Not unless there is a hurricane blowing out there that no one told us about."

Ruth sprang to the window. She flung open the curtains and squealed, "Viola Lee!"

Viola Lee ran. She bounded through the front parlor, her dressing gown and veil streaming behind her. She ran down the porch steps, and stopped. She held her hand to her heaving chest and the veil wrapped around her.

James stood, a tanned hand on the gate, and looked up at her like he was seeing a vision. A dimpled smile covered his face, and he shook his head. "I remembered you were pretty," he said, his lilting voice a mixture of his Appalachian forefathers and the soft cadence of his Florida-born cousins, "but I misremembered that you were beautiful."

He strode forward, held his arms out, and Viola Lee stumbled into his arms, blinded by the veil that had wrapped itself across her face. James gently loosened the veil and kissed her full on the lips.

"Oh, James!" she said, pulling away and pressing her face against the softness of his blue chambray shirt. "You are here!"

"Yep," he said. "I'm here."

Hand in hand they climbed up the porch stairs, and Ruth and Mary Scarlett untangled Viola Lee's veil.

James said, "There's someone I want you to meet."

They looked to where he pointed, and Viola Lee saw a young man with James's eyes and build, but instead of the blonde curly hair that sat atop James's head like cotton, his hair was dark brown, of the same shade as Viola Lee's.

"It's nice to meet you," Viola Lee said, holding out her hand.

"He's my brother, Roy."

"He didn't want me coming alone," James said, speaking for Roy, who seemed too shy to utter a sentence.

Viola Lee smiled warmly at him, and he replied with a shy smile of his own. She liked him immediately. "James has told me a lot about you," she said. "I'm so pleased I've finally gotten to meet you."

"My pleasure," Roy mumbled, his words polite, his face bright red.

"Now you young ones run along and make ready for the wedding," Mary Scarlett said. "Guests should be arriving in a couple of hours, and I want you all scrubbed and ready. I've got a lot to do, and I don't need you all standing here gawking at each other and getting in my way."

They all laughed.

She hung a "Closing at Noon for Wedding" sign on the door of her dry goods store. She turned slowly and met Viola Lee's eyes.

Viola Lee smiled so big it felt like her cheeks reached right up to her eyes. Mary Scarlett nodded and, ever so slowly, returned her smile.

Ruth and Viola Lee turned to go into the house, and Roy and James walked around to the back of the house, where Mary Scarlett insisted the two of them bathe and prepare for guests.

The gate squeaked again and Viola Lee looked out the window.

Her eyes grew wide, and her heart began to thump when the gate opened and first Annie Laura, then Louise, and finally a shriveled old woman walked through. They weren't dressed for the wedding.

Chapter 25

Viola Lee's heart thumped. She looked over to her mother and saw Mary Scarlett squinting to make out who the visitors were.

Annie Laura came first, held her hand out to the group behind her to stop them from coming forward.

A frown collapsed Mary Scarlett's lips, and then her brows drew together in anger.

Annie Laura stopped halfway down the sidewalk, waiting, it seemed, for an invitation to move forward. Viola Lee stepped in between them, afraid of what Mary Scarlett would say.

But it was James who broke the tension. "Annie Laura!" he said, strode forward, hugged her, presented her to Viola Lee and Mary Scarlett, John Sebring, and Ruth. "This woman," he said, "saved my life," and his voice broke.

Viola Lee hastened down the porch steps and took Annie's hand. She squeezed it, happy to see her.

"No," James said. "Wait. I need to tell this story. You don't know?" he said, asking Viola Lee.

"No," she said.

James cast a glance back at the two women behind Annie. "And from the looks on your faces, you don't know either. Annie Laura, you've not told anyone?" he asked.

"Water under the bridge," she said. "I had other things needed doing."

"What's he talking about, Mama?" Louise asked.

Viola Lee studied Louise with the eyes of someone who might meet the two of them for the first time. Would a stranger know immediately that Louise was her sister?. Louise was taller than Viola Lee, had a widow's peak in her brown hair, the same color as Viola Lee's. But the eyes were the same, as was the set of their jaws. No one could deny it. They were sisters.

Viola Lee caught Louise's eye, smiled shyly at her. Louise looked down at the ground, back up again, and smiled at Viola Lee.

They might could be friends. Maybe not here in Grassy Glade, Florida, with Mary Scarlett looking on, but somewhere.

There was an awkward silence, and Viola Lee realized everyone was waiting on Mary Scarlett to invite their guests inside.

Viola Lee saw something working on Mary Scarlett's face. John Sebring lay a hand on Mary Scarlett's arm, and she shook it off. She squeezed her eyes shut, and if she had been a praying woman, Viola Lee would have sworn she was praying.

But Viola Lee knew that Mary Scarlett was not struggling with Jesus, unless some miracle had occurred that she didn't know about.

Mary Scarlett was struggling with herself. She'd spent Viola Lee's lifetime making Viola Lee believe not through words, but through glances and silences, that Viola Lee's birth mother was not the kind of woman she would welcome readily to her table.

And yet, here she was. And it would be a blatant show of bad manners not to welcome her into her house and invite her to her table.

The silence continued.

The women gazed at one another.

Mary Scarlett swallowed, like she was wetting her mouth to say something. But she didn't.

Viola Lee felt sick, wanted to speak, but words wouldn't come. Annie Laura loosened her hand from Viola Lee's and stepped forward. Stepped in front of Viola Lee and James. And stood in between them and Mary Scarlett.

Mary Scarlett stared down at her. A gentle afternoon breeze stirred Mary Scarlett's skirt. She patted it down as if the wind might lift her up and carry her down to face Annie Laura.

The woman whose baby she stole.

They waited.

Annie Laura spoke, softly, so that even Viola Lee had to strain to hear her. "The years have been good to you, Sally."

Sally. Only John Sebring called her Sally. It was the name from her childhood, the pet name that she'd long grown out of, or so she told Viola Lee when Viola Lee asked.

Mary Scarlett moved to speak, but Annie Laura held her hand up to stop her. "No, don't even say it. It's not true and you know it. I have worked my land until the sun robbed me of my youth. But," she said, wryly, "youth isn't all it's supposed to be, or so I've found. I would do a lot of things different with what I know now."

"But we don't get to do that, do we?" Mary Scarlett said.

Viola Lee studied her mother. And suddenly she realized that the anger that had been on Mary Scarlett's face had been replaced by a grief so deep that lines Viola Lee had never noticed appeared in her face.

Mary Scarlett looked old.

"What's done is done, Sally," Annie Laura said. "And I hold no hard feelings against you. You did what you thought was the right thing."

She let the words soak into Mary Scarlett, who closed her eyes again.

Mary Scarlett licked her lips. Looked down. Shaded her face with one hand. Massaged her forehead. Allowed her hand to cradle her forehead for a moment and then looked up.

"I'm sorry, Annie Laura. I am."

Annie Laura stood, silent.

"You are welcome to this wedding," Mary Scarlett said. "It's right that you should be here to see her married."

Annie Laura shook her head. "That's not what I'm here about," she said.

John Sebring wrapped an arm around Mary Scarlett's shoulders. "Come on in, Annie Laura," he said. "It's hot out here. Let's sit around the table and talk for a little while before we get these two young'uns married."

His cheery voice broke the tension, but not the silence, and they moved inside like birds making a "V" formation, traveling to the destination that would sustain life.

Chapter 26

Annie Laura couldn't help the sense of dread she felt walking into Mary Scarlett's house. It wasn't about Mary Scarlett herself, though the Lord knew she had plenty to dread being around her. She could forgive her for taking Viola Lee. Mary Scarlett had been blind to Walter's shortcomings her entire life. She had been his adoring little sister and believed everything he said. Annie Laura had long ago forgiven Mary Scarlett. She wasn't about to carry that kind of poisonous anger around with her. But forgiving wasn't the same as forgetting. She wasn't a fool. She had grown stronger because of it. Strong enough to know she would never allow herself to be taken advantage of again.

No, her dread had everything to do with the joy on Viola Lee's face as she held James Stewart's hand, looking up at him adoringly. The blush on her cheeks and matching blush on his told Annie Laura all she needed to know about how deeply in love they were.

She walked into the cool darkness of Mary Scarlett's parlor, saw the intricately crocheted antimacassars adorning the backs of a silk sofa, and two matching chairs. She took in the photo album, with its pink silk cover, that she knew was filled with tintypes of Sally's mother, father, and grandparents.

Annie Laura had pored over them as a child with Mary Scarlett, each imagining the lives of those seemingly ancient ancestors. Of course, they weren't ancient at all, probably only in their thirties or forties, but to two young girls in their early teens, they were ancient. Annie Laura smiled with the memory, and laid her hand on the pink album, stroking it gently. She was thankful she had not had the gift of seeing into their future, seeing the events that would rip their friendship apart as messily as corn shucked from its protective covering, silk hanging like hair in messy disarray.

Life changed you, that was for sure. Annie Laura looked up at Mary Scarlett, her hand still on the pink album, and nodded a greeting. Mary Scarlett was watching her, the look on her face piercing, but at the same time searching. Was she looking for the friend from long ago? Too much water had passed under the bridge for that friendship to be.

Everyone else filed into the kitchen and Annie Laura and Mary Scarlett were left alone.

"I'm sorry, Annie," Mary Scarlett said, her eyes downcast, her face filled with shame. "I'm sorry for believing Walter over you. He's not changed. He never will."

"I forgive you. I forgave you long ago. That anger nearly killed me. I couldn't keep carrying it around."

Mary Scarlett looked up at Annie, and now the tears filled her eyes and spilled over. "He told me you didn't want her. He told me that the land was more important to you than the baby, that after your daddy died, it was all you cared about. He said that without the land you couldn't take care of the baby anyway, and you needed to be separated from the baby as quickly as possible. You didn't even need to know where the baby had gone to."

"And you believed him," Annie Laura said.

"I believed him because I wanted to believe him," she said. "All those years I kept wanting to believe Walter's lies. He has a way about him, makes me feel sorry for him, even where there is no good reason to. And this lie, I wanted to believe most of all."

Mary Scarlett fell silent. Annie Laura waited. Mary Scarlett's normal grim-faced proclamations had taken a turn. Her face looked like the face of one of Annie's children when someone had hurt them—innocent, pained, and beseeching.

"I believed him because I knew I could never provide John Sebring with a baby. I desperately wanted him to love me like he had loved Maggie, and I thought a baby would do it. It didn't. Does Leonard still love you, Annie? Does he love holding you in his arms?"

"We went through a long dry spell. John Sebring loves you, Mary Scarlett. He is just afraid to show it. You don't act like you need him, and he needs to know that you do."

"I don't need him. That's the problem," Mary Scarlett said, wiping her hands over her apron. "I've never needed him. Needing a man is a weakness my mama had, and I'll never fall into that same weakness. Never."

Mary Scarlett's grimace told Annie Laura that her words were truthful and that the marriage would continue just as it was.

"I understand," Annie Laura said. "But, girl, there is no weakness in love. There is no weakness in needing your man. It's how God made us, so that we could work together."

"God?" Mary Scarlett said. "Horse piss. He's never been there when I needed him. Where was he when my mama took her own life? Where was he...," and then she broke down. "Where was he that awful night of the fire?" she sobbed. "If he is so good, why didn't he help you? Why did he let that happen?"

Annie Laura felt the tears smart in her own eyes. She understood that anger against God, had nursed it herself for a long time. Why had God let it happen? She would never know the answer to that. But she laid a hand on Mary Scarlett and offered her the only comfort she'd been able to find for herself. "Jesus told us that he wasn't the prince of this world—this world is filled with evil and hurt and pain. But he said he'd leave us a comforter, the holy spirit. God can protect my heart, but not my body, when evil folks choose to enact evil upon me."

"What do you mean God can protect your heart?" she asked.

"God gives me a peace that helps me notice the small things around me that are worth giving thanks for. And then my worry becomes a peace that I don't always understand."

"And how long does that last?" Mary Scarlett asked, skeptical.

"Well, you know the story of the manna?" Annie Laura asked.

"Yes, the children of Israel tried to save it, but it rotted. But God gave them new manna every day," Mary Scarlett responded. She knew her Bible.

"That's the way it is. I have to seek it anew every morning. And then, I have to go out and think on ways to make the people around me feel loved, which is easier with some than it is with others."

"Humph," Mary Scarlett said. "Sounds like a lot of work without much payoff."

Annie Laura laughed. "It sounds that way, but it's not. Try it for a few days. You'll see."

Viola Lee appeared at the kitchen door. "Are you two coming?" she asked.

"I expect so," Mary Scarlett replied.

In the kitchen, John Sebring offered his guests biscuits and ham. The wedding sweets would be saved for after the wedding, but there was plenty of lemonade and he shared that freely.

Annie Laura didn't eat. She watched Mary eat her fill and then motioned to her, reminding her of the grim mission they were on.

Mary stood up. "Come on, young'un," she said, pointing to James. And, after a pause, to Roy, his brother.

Annie Laura stood and went with them. Mary Scarlett rose, as did John Sebring and Viola Lee, but Annie Laura held her hand up to stop them. "No," she said. "This is private business. We'll be back in a little while."

She swallowed, and she was certain her face was as pained as her heart.

Chapter 27

They stood on the wide back porch, James and Roy studying Mary as if they waited for her to tell them what they'd done wrong.

"What is this about?" James asked.

"I can't explain, son," Annie Laura said. "But I need you to trust me. This is important what we're doing here."

Mary edged closer to James, put her ancient hand on his back. "I need you to lift your shirt, son," she said.

"I would rather not, ma'am," he said.

Mary looked at Annie.

"She needs to look at something, James. You can trust her. It's okay."

James squeezed his jaw, the muscles working on the sides of his cheeks.

"I would rather not, ma'am," he said.

"What's the matter, brother?" Roy asked. "She only wants to look at your back."

James shook his head.

"Here," Roy said, "let me lift your shirt."

"No," James said.

The four of them stood in a frozen silence.

"It's for Viola Lee, James. Do it for Viola Lee," Annie Laura said.

James's face squeezed as if in pain. Finally he relented, allowed Roy to help Mary lift the back of his shirt.

"Good Lord in heaven," Mary said, her voice expressing the horror that Annie Laura had feared.

Annie's heart sank. So it was. James was Viola Lee's brother. They could not marry. Annie Laura tried to think of how she would break the news to Viola Lee. The Lord would have to guide her. She didn't have the words in her head and certainly not in her mouth.

"Who did this to you?" Mary asked. "What animal did this to you?"

"Brother!" Roy said. "You tell me who did this and I'm going to beat the shit out of him."

He looked around, embarrassed, at Annie Laura and Mary "Beggin' your pardon, ma'ams," Roy said. "Did you know about this?" he asked Mary.

"No," she said, shaking her head. "I didn't."

"Then what wuz you looking for?" Roy asked.

James looked at her, curious.

"I wouldn't be able to find it even if it were there," Mary said. "His back looks like pounded meat."

Annie Laura closed her eyes. Of course. She'd forgotten all about the beatings the men received at the lumber camp. She remembered the poor man strung up on the tree whom she had insisted on the lumber boss bringing down.

Now they would never know if James was the brother. What should she do? Allow the two their ignorance? *Dear Lord,* she prayed, *give me guidance.*

"I need some salve. Otherwise, this back is never going to heal," Mary said. "Ask Mary Scarlett where she keeps it."

Roy went inside after the salve.

"Ma'am," James said, "could you tell me how you knew about my back? Was it Miss Annie Laura who told you?"

"I didn't know about your back," Mary said. "I was looking for something completely other. But I'm glad I seen your back. I'm going to doctor on it some, make it so that it doesn't sting so bad. And make it so that it doesn't seep through your wedding shirt."

"That would be nice," James said.

"How did you keep that hidden from your brother?" Annie Laura asked.

James smiled a half smile. "Roy doesn't see so good," he said. "As long as I was a few feet away from him, all he sees is a blur. Now, up close he can see real good. Makes him a sorry shot, but a fine meat-skinner. And you ain't never tasted a squirrel stew like that boy can put together."

The knot in Annie's throat wouldn't go away.

"Here, now," Roy said, returning with the salve. "You want me to hold up his shirt so you can dress his back?" he asked.

"Yes, son," Mary said. "That would be mighty helpful."

Roy held up his shirt, and Annie Laura began walking inside. She had to tell Mary Scarlett. She needed to get some insight as to how to carry on here. She didn't feel right letting them marry not knowing.

She walked toward the back door, her feet like lead. She lay her hand on the brass doorknob, opened the heavy wood door. Someone was on the other side. Whoever it was pushed the door open, hard, nearly knocking Annie Laura down. Roy turned to see who it was and his face whitened.

"He's here again!" Roy called out, his voice panicked.

James turned to see who it was. "You get the hell out of here!" James yelled. James jerked away from Mary, ran down the stairs, and pushed a wobbly man to the ground. Before anyone could move, James sat on the man's chest, pummeling his face.

"Brother," Roy said, "stop it! You are going to kill him."

"It's what he deserves," James said. "This is for what you did to my mother," he said, and punched the man. "And this is for what you did to my brother," he said, and punched the man again. The sound of bone cracking wafted over the yard.

"Here, what's this?" John Sebring came running down the porch, Roy alongside him.

They pulled James off the man. James struggled against them.

"What makes you think you can show your face around here?" James bellowed. "What gives you the right?"

The man struggled up, blood pouring from his nose, a gash above his eyebrow. Mary and Annie Laura ran down to the man, and Mary helped him up.

Annie Laura shrank back in horror. John Sebring grabbed James's arm.

When Mary saw Annie's face, she dropped him back to the ground.

"Why can't you leave me alone?" Roy bellowed.

James struggled, but John Sebring held him close.

"Send someone after the sheriff," John Sebring called out.

Mary Scarlett nodded without pausing.

"He's the reason Roy can't see good," James said. "The bastard hurt Roy once when he was a little boy, and I wasn't around to help him." The rage in James' otherwise placid face that curled his lip and widened his eyes told Annie Laura they had best hold tight to James or he would kill Walter Blakely.

"He says he's my daddy," Roy whispered.

Walter Blakely stood, wavered, and fell down again. He sat up, pointed at Viola Lee and Roy, and with what might have been a smirk had his face not been rearranged by James' fist, he said, "Two of my children right here. She's one of my little girls. They're all around here," he rambled. "I've done what the good Lord called me to do: 'Be fruitful and multiply.' And so I have." His high-pitched cackling laugh was silenced by a sudden gust of wind.

John Sebring let loose of James and strode toward Walter Blakely. "I'm escorting you off of my property for the last time, Blakely," he said. "The next time you set foot on my property will be the day you set your first foot in hell."

Blakely continued laughing, and John Sebring jerked him by his shirt collar and disappeared with him around the side of the house.

Roy looked at Viola Lee, realization dawning on his face. He walked over to her, took her tiny hand in his, and said, "We done nothing wrong. We ain't got nothing to be 'shamed of. He's the only shameful creature here." And Roy spat in the direction of Walter Blakely.

The county sheriff appeared, handcuffs ready. "This time I've got enough to put you away for life."

Blakely's mocking laughter was silenced.

The sheriff cuffed him and let him away.

Annie Laura looked over at Mary the glimmer of a smile in her eyes.

Mary walked over and lifted Roy's shirt.

Annie Laura planted a kiss on the cornflower-shaped birthmark on the boy's back.

He jerked away. "What was that about?" he asked.

"That, son," Annie Laura said, "was the kiss of life."

Chapter 28

It wasn't the wedding party Viola Lee imagined. There were no friends dressed in their Sunday best. But Ruth was there, and Roy, James's brother and, apparently, her own. There was her birth mother, Annie, and her grandmother and her half-sister, Louise.

"Mama and Daddy may come looking for me," Ruth said, but with her chin out she continued, "I don't care. I'm staying here. You're my best friend in the world, Viola Lee, and I'm not missing your wedding."

Viola Lee looked up at Ruth's troubled face and worried that it might be too much for her, this worry, this going against what she knew her mama and daddy wanted, but the set of Ruth's jaw told her there was no talking her out of it, that no matter what, she was staying for the wedding.

"Do you have a dress I could borrow?" Ruth asked. "If I go home for mine, I'm afraid they'll make me stay."

They hunted through Viola Lee's closet. Viola Lee glanced out the window, afraid that Ruth's parents would show up, afraid that Ruth would be forced to go home and miss her wedding.

They came up with a pretty dress with an embroidered pink netting overlay and a matching hat. Mary Scarlett had made it for Viola Lee—it had been her Easter dress—ordering the netting from England and painstakingly embroidering over all of it. It was beautiful.

Ruth slipped it over her head, and they both giggled.

The dress was a few inches too short.

"Just wait till those gossipy biddies at church see this," Ruth said, laughing, pointing to her exposed ankles.

Viola Lee laughed. "Not a single soul here is from the church other than you and me, and I'll not judge."

Ruth wore her brogans with the dress; they were all she had, and Viola Lee's foot was too tiny for her to even consider a pair of her slippers.

The girls took turns braiding their hair. Ruth placed the veil on Viola Lee's head, and then held her cheeks between her hands.

"You are the most beautiful bride I've ever seen in my life. I wouldn't have missed this day for anything."

Viola Lee's throat tightened. She looked at Ruth and hugged her tight. "You'll come visit me, won't you?"

"Of course I will!" Ruth said. "You better have a spare bedroom in that first Panama City cabin you build!"

Viola Lee laughed. Oh, how she longed for Ruth to come with her. If Ruth could find someone to marry, willing to live in Panama City, her world would be perfect.

Ruth took her hand. "Come on, girl, before my parents get here and snatch me away."

Viola Lee took her hand and picked up the flower bouquet from where she had set it on the washstand.

She opened the door and took a deep breath. "Oh, my!" she said.

Mary Scarlett festooned the parlor with flowers and gauze, creating the perfect setting for a fairytale wedding. Azaleas sat in every available container. Two bolts of gauze hung from the ceiling like a gentle cloud. The electric ceiling light glowed magically behind it. There was an archway set up, made from gauze that Viola Lee was about to walk through. Another gauze archway set at the opposite end of the room, near the fireplace, and the mantle was filled with glowing candles. The preacher stood smiling at her. James's back was to her.

Then, he turned.

For just a moment, Ruth stood in between them, but Viola Lee walked forward slowly as if they had practiced a million times. There was no music other than the song in Viola Lee's heart, but it was enough.

Ruth cast a nervous glance to the door, but no parents were there threatening to bring her home.

Viola Lee whispered a prayer for their marriage before looking at James, his blue eyes shining, their bold color piercing

She walked past Louise and Mary, and stopped at Annie Laura, gave her a big hug, and whispered into her ear, "I love you!"

Annie Laura trembled, her eyes grew bright, and she hugged her tightly.

Viola Lee had almost reached John Sebring and Mary Scarlett. She smiled broadly at them.

And the iron gate squeaked.

Viola Lee paused and looked beneath the gauze and out the front window.

It was Ruth's parents.

Viola Lee froze.

They were dressed for church and didn't look the least bit angry. In Mrs. Merritt's arm was something soft and white.

They hastily climbed up the porch and walked through the open front door.

"We aren't too late!" she heard Mrs. Merritt exclaim. "We're going to get to see our Viola Lee marry!"

Viola Lee smiled and gave them a moment to move into the house before walking to Mary Scarlett and whispering, "I love you, Mama. Thank you for making my day perfect!"

Tears trickled down Mary Scarlett's face. John Sebring took Viola Lee's arm and walked her to the makeshift altar.

Mary Scarlett had fashioned a cross out of cypress and festooned it with azaleas, dainty whites, and ivy, the symbol of life and hope.

"Who gives this woman in marriage?" the pastor asked.

"Her mothers and I," John Sebring said, and winked at Viola Lee.

Viola Lee smiled. It was fitting.

James held his arm out for Viola Lee to clasp, and when she did, the warmth of his arm, the softness of his shirt, the clean smell of him enveloped her sense and she felt dizzy. She looked up into his blue eyes and stumbled a tiny bit. The muscles in his strong arm tightened, giving her a steady anchor to keep herself from falling.

He looked down at her and smiled. She felt so tiny beside him. But she knew this about James Stewart: his arm was strong, as was his soul and his spirit. This was for life.

—THE END—

Acknowledgements

It's nearly impossible to name the dozens of friends and family who have helped make the dream of this book turn into reality. My first debt of thanks goes to the storytellers in my family who have delightfully and mysteriously teased me with half-truths and almost complete stories leaving me to do the research that may or may not have filled out the truth. But, since this is a novel and not a memoir, I was free to fill in the blanks by reimagining the truth. My mother, my father, my aunts, my grandmothers, my cousins, my sister and brothers have all added their flavor to this story.

Once the story became a draft, my good friends, the Cheshires helped me believe in my story. A special thank you to Dr. Marty who reeled me in and brought me back to the solid path of writing about my kin. Thank you also to Mark, Tony, Carole, Ruth and Rich who have all helped me write better.

Thank you to my fellow writers, Karen Zacharias and Michael Morris, for your friendship and for making sure this novel found a home.

A special thanks to Elizabeth Stuckey-French's graduate novel revision seminar at FSU. Your input into a very early draft of this book was invaluable. It would never have made it to print without you.

Thank you to the wonderful folks at Mercer, Marc and Marsha, for taking a chance on me and seeing the project through with great patience.

Thank you to my husband, Hal, who in the earliest stages of this book tromped around cemeteries and waded through countless courthouse documents with a great deal of patience.

Thank you to my nephew, Chuck, for helping me work through kinks in the plot and who was always willing to listen.

Thank you to my son, Robbie, who reminded me that art is a gift to be valued and encouraged me to pursue my dream, draft-by-draft.

Thank you to my daughter, Jenny, for listening carefully enough to make sense of the story.

I could never have gotten through the final stages of the editing process without my good friends at the Office of Advancement at Florida State University Panama City. Their generosity with time and their infinite patience in the face of my deadlines is something I hope one day to be able to pay forward. Thank you Becky, Erin, Helen and Erica for reading, editing, and helping me rethink and polish. Thank you Tasha and Mary Beth for being supportive.

And most of all, thank you to my cousin, Sandy Moore, whose unflagging persistence pulled redemptive truth from the silence of shame.